Redemption

A Regency Romance

by

Jaimey Grant

Redemption
A Regency Romance
by Jaimey Grant

Cover design by Laura J Miller
www.anauthorsart.com

Published by TreasureLine Publishing
www.treasurelinebooks.com

First published September 2008
Third Edition
EAN13: 978-1-61752-168-3

Printed in the United States of America.

Also by Jaimey Grant

Connected Regencies:

Honor
Betrayal
Deception
Entangled (Spellbound)
Heartless
Redemption

Short Stories:

My Lady Coward: An Episodic Regency Romance
The 11th Commandment: A Serial Regency Romance
Assassin's Keeper / Survival in Unlocked: Ten "Key" Tales
The Dragon's Birth (fantasy)

Redemption

TREASURELINE PUBLISHING

One

England 1821

Darius Prestwich stepped off the boat, one of the many owned by his cousin, Sir Adam Prestwich. He swung his pack over his shoulder and looked around at all the people milling about the city of Portsmouth. People coming and going, crewmen shouting, an overall sense of order amidst the chaos.

As passengers scurried about, Dare's eyes scanned the crowd. One person in particular snared his gaze and he stared, hardly daring to believe his own eyes. If he didn't know better, he'd think it was Adam. Upon closer inspection, he realized it was indeed his cousin accompanied by a heavily veiled woman of diminutive stature and a large young man who stood out due to his very size.

He thought of approaching them but he was held back by one of the captains employed by his cousin. "I say, Mr.

Dare, are you off to see Sir Adam?"

Dare turned to the burly man and replied, "Yes, Captain Blake, as a matter of fact I am. He stands just over yonder." Dare tipped his head toward the little group. "Was there something you'd like me to make known to him?"

"Let him know the *Bonny Mae* went down. I just received word this minute."

Dare stood very still. It was the third ship they'd lost in twice as many months. Adam's shipping business couldn't stand much more loss. "Are you sure?"

"Sure as I'm standin' here, Mr. Dare."

"Any survivors?"

The captain shook his head sadly. "Nay, lad, none. The ship disappeared, too, just like the others."

Dare shook his head. It was a mystery he thought might never be solved. "Who imparted the message to you, Captain Blake?"

"It was young Jimmy Smith. His papa sails for that there Lord Penryn."

Dare gazed at the ruddy captain thoughtfully. He had heard of Lord Penryn before. The man was an enigma and never strayed far from his home in Cornwall. He also happened to be Adam's biggest shipping rival.

"Very well. I'll let my cousin know." He turned to

walk away but the captain stopped him again.

"When is he goin' to make you a cap'n, young man?" Captain Blake asked kindly.

"That, my dear captain, is very much up to Sir Adam," replied Dare. He saluted the captain in a mocking gesture and walked away.

He was not altogether surprised when he observed Adam heading in his direction, his companions following close behind. He stopped and waited for them.

Holding out his hand in greeting, he said, "Adam, well met. I need to speak with you."

Adam smiled in greeting, shaking his hand. His oddly colored gray-green eyes glinted with a warning that Dare couldn't begin to understand.

Then he glanced at the woman—a lady to judge by her garb—and the young man and wondered if his cousin was aiding an elopement. He returned his gaze to Adam, one black brow lifted in faintly mocking inquiry.

Adam ushered him to one side, neglecting to introduce him to the couple. "Dare, I need a favor."

Dare held up a hand. "First, let me impart my information. Captain Blake informed me that the *Bonny Mae* went down."

Adam's brow furrowed. "How many is that now?"

"Three in six months."

"Damn. Is there any clue as to what is happening to them?"

"Every man has been lost and the ships seem to disappear from the face of the earth. It appears to be true of the *Bonny Mae* as well. I will look into the matter at great length when I get the chance of it."

"Good man." Adam looked back at his companions uneasily. "I have another favor to ask of you."

Dare listened with growing disbelief as Adam explained the situation in which he found himself. As soon as Adam finished, he said, "You must be jesting! You want me to squire a passel of females around during the Season? Have you lost your mind? What do I know of Society? I haven't attended the Season in…well, ever. I can't possibly —"

"Miles has, dammit, and he will be there too. Please just do as I ask and leave me to get this latest problem out of my hair."

Dare reluctantly agreed and watched his cousin walk away. He swore under his breath and headed into the town.

Miles watched Lady Brianna Prestwich pace much in the same way her cousin, the Earl of Greville, was wont to do. Lady Bri only did so when she was particularly disturbed, however. Lord Greville had a tendency to do it all the time.

"My lady, I wish you would stop and tell me what I am to do. I cannot read your mind and although I have been here for all of fifteen minutes, you have yet to tell me why. I do not want to sound rude but I have several things to accomplish for Adam."

Bri stopped pacing, giving her husband's cousin a look of disgust. She had ever had little patience for strictly organized people and Miles Prestwich was one of the worst.

"You can oblige me for a minute or two, Miles. I'm sure whatever it is Adam has set for you can wait."

She started moving again and Miles feared he might develop a headache to match the crick that was swiftly developing in his neck.

She threw him an annoyed glare. "And I told you to call me Bri. Do I have to make Adam order you to make use of the god…*blasted* name?"

Miles allowed a tiny smile to play about his lips. He was positive Lady Prestwich cleaned up her language out of deference to him. She did make life very interesting, to be sure.

"Here is my problem, Miles," Bri said finally, stopping again to stare at him steadily. "Adam has gone out of town to take care of some things and it is left up to Rory and I to scotch a few rumors that seem to have crept up on us when we weren't looking. We need you to squire us to balls and parties so we can gossip."

"What of Lord Greville?"

"He went with Adam." Bri favored him with a look that implied he should have known that.

Perhaps he should have. "Very well," responded Miles. He really did not want to but perhaps he would see a certain lady again by traveling in the same circles as her.

"Thank you, Miles," Lady Prestwich said with an unusually hefty dose of sickeningly sweet charm. "You may go now."

Miles bowed and departed. He closed the drawing room doors behind him and returned to the study at the back of the mansion.

He sat down at the large mahogany desk and started sorting through the papers lying there. After several minutes of pointless shuffling, he realized what he was doing and stopped. He had no time to daydream about a pair of heavenly blue eyes, a pert nose, and soft blond curls.

Dare was admitted into Lockwood House in Berkeley Square without much fuss and ushered into the drawing room. The butler, West, announced him and he was faced with his cousin's wife for the first time. He thought she was beautiful, of course, with her deep red hair and emerald green eyes, but there was something in her expression, in her bearing, perhaps even the look in her eyes that made him very thankful she was Adam's wife and not his own.

"Lady Prestwich, it is a pleasure to finally meet you," he said with an elegant bow.

She said nothing for a moment, her eyes sweeping his form in quite the rudest manner he'd ever experienced. Not a hint of embarrassment marred her beautiful features when she once again settled her gaze on his face. She stared for several moments, her eyes narrowing. Then, "It's your eyes."

"Excuse me?" he inquired, wondering if perhaps he'd missed something vitally important.

"Your eyes. Miles's are not as dark a blue as yours. Lovely. I shall have no trouble telling you apart even if you cut your hair and style it just like his." She gestured to a chair. "Please sit. We should get acquainted."

Dare glanced ruefully at his travel-stained clothing. "Perhaps after I've had time to refresh myself, my lady."

"Now don't you go starting that, too. I have just this moment told your brother to stop calling me that and I will tell you the same thing. I have a name. It is Brianna. I would appreciate it if you would call me Bri. *Lady Prestwich*, *Lady Rothsmere*, and *my lady* are just so stuffy, do you not think?"

"Indeed, Bri," he replied with a charming smile. "I will endeavor to remember. In the meantime, you must call me Dare. I will answer to nothing else."

Bri smiled, her striking beauty almost blinding. "Wonderful. I can tell we will get along famously." With that, she dismissed him to clean up.

Dare was led to a handsome apartment on the third floor, one of many suites reserved for family use. He appreciated the rather masculine furnishings and was pleased to note the water closet that was just off one end of the dressing room. It had been quite some time since he'd visited Lockwood House and he was impressed with Adam's improvements.

He made use of the wash room and changed into fresh

clothes, pulling on worn but comfortable doeskin breeches, a loose linen shirt, and a jacket of navy blue. He left his shirt open at the neck and tied a simple belcher neckerchief around his tanned throat.

As he left his rooms, he hoped Bri would not mind his casual attire. He was not about to dress in the restricting clothing demanded by Society until he absolutely had to— and even then he would balk at every restraining article.

He knew he would have to find a valet soon, as well, and he really didn't care one. He had become used to having his privacy and it was something he now closely guarded.

Instead of returning to the drawing room on the first floor, Dare decided to do a little exploring. He eased his way past the open doors of the room containing Bri and hurried down the rest of the stairs. He supposed Miles was about somewhere and if he knew his twin at all, he was willing to bet he was in the study poring over paperwork.

Dare shuddered. He hated paperwork. In fact, he could barely read and that suited him just fine. He had no use for books or newspapers and less use for writing.

Miles, on the other hand, had a flair for making sense of chaotic offices, studies, and libraries and simply thrived on literature. He usually had his nose in some book or other or his hands in papers that made no sense to anyone sane. Another shudder snaked through Dare's body at the mere thought of organizing anything.

Making another turn, Dare faced a closed door. He was willing to bet he faced the study, as it was furthest from the noise of the street and house traffic. He pushed it open and walked in.

Miles looked up with a guilty flush, thinking it was Bri who had caught him daydreaming. He frowned when he saw his wandering twin.

Dare grinned, his face appearing even more handsome than normal. "Please, Miles, your excitement over seeing me again after all these years is unbecoming in a man. Restrain yourself." He crossed his arms over his chest and advanced into the room, gazing about in interest.

Miles frowned even more heavily at his brother's levity but remained silent for the moment. Then he noticed Dare's choice of garb. "What the devil are you wearing?"

Dare looked down with an expression of feigned wonder on his face. "Oh, dear Father in heaven! I'm wearing clothes! I left my room naked. Where did these come from?" He pulled at his shirt, making it billow out away from his muscular chest. His look of bafflement was something to behold.

Miles almost smiled at Dare's playacting, reminded of many childhood escapades. Instead, he gave him a stern look. "You are dressed far too casual for London and our cousin's home, Dare. What if someone calls on Bri and sees you dressed like that? You could ruin all of our social cache in just one sitting."

"What if, shwat if," remarked Dare carelessly. "I will wear what I want until I am forced to go about in Society. And if the ladies who visit will be frightened by my dress I will simply hide until they go away."

"Will you cut your hair?"

That wiped the grin off Dare's face. "Why should I?"

"You look like a pirate, Dare. All you lack is the eyepatch."

A gleam of interest lit Dare's expressive face. "Indeed. I'll look into that."

Miles released an exasperated breath. "As you will," he muttered, wondering why he even tried to change his brother. It was a thankless task and never successful.

"I've often wondered the same, brother," Dare uttered softly. "Trying to change someone who is equally determined not to is ever frustrating."

Miles shook his head, a trifle aghast at his twin's unnerving perspicacity.

Several minutes passed with Miles once again poring over his paperwork and his twin prowling around, poking his fingers into everything like a curious child. Miles felt like a father sometimes when he was with Dare and it was not a feeling he enjoyed considering he was the younger of the two—by twelve minutes.

"If you are going to hang about, Dare, do something productive, please."

Dare stopped prowling and stared at Miles. "What do you suggest?" He moved across the room and stood looking over his twin's shoulder. "Do you have party invitations that need addressed?" he asked impudently, knowing this was not an activity that fell under Miles's jurisdiction. "I assure you, should I do so, all the invitations would go astray resulting in some unsavory characters arriving for the ball...or rout...or breakfast...or whatever."

He paused, one finger on his chin in a pose of thinking that Miles knew was feigned. "Why do they call it a breakfast? They never start until three in the afternoon and go until all hours." The look he bestowed on his brother positively begged for an answer.

Miles managed to contain his annoyance. He had a difficult time dealing with Dare's lackadaisical way of life. The man was eight-and-twenty years old. It was time for him to grow up and stop acting like life was a game.

Dare knew how his attitude annoyed Miles and secretly reveled in it. Their relationship was a constant struggle between comedy and drama, Dare preferring to laugh at the bumps in the road of life and Miles preferring to analyze and configure everything life tossed in his path. The very thought of taking life seriously wearied Dare to the point he was afraid he might have to retire to his room for a two-week nap.

The slightly elder of the two identical gentlemen resumed his place behind his brother's shoulder, shamelessly perusing the paper currently on the top of the stack. He was intrigued to note that a lady's name seemed to be scrawled across the page with many flourishes. Did his brother have a *tendre* for someone?

"Dare, do you mind?" snapped Miles. He jerked the paper out of the other man's line of sight. He was more annoyed with himself than his brother but the way Dare was hovering made him edgy.

Dare's ready grin flashed again. "No, I don't mind."

"Get out!"

Laughing, Dare left Miles to his papers. He crossed the hall and went back upstairs. As he moved past the drawing room, Lady Prestwich stepped out. He stopped.

"I wondered if perhaps you were lost," remarked Bri with a smile. "Then I heard Miles yell and I assumed it was a little brotherly squabble."

"You were right." Dare smiled. "So tell me all the news. I have not heard anything to date."

Two

Lady Genevieve Northwicke stared at the young man with feigned incomprehension. She fluttered her eyelashes and gave him such an ingenuous look that he felt quite intelligent, which was just what she wanted him to think. The poor young captain had neither wit nor looks and Jenny did not have the heart to puncture his bubble of self-importance.

Finally growing tired of her feigned stupidity, she smiled and asked, "Captain Carter, would you be so good as to escort me to my sister. I do believe she is signaling me."

"Of course, Lady Genevieve." The captain bowed and held out his arm.

Jenny placed her hand on his arm and followed him across the crowded ballroom. She managed to keep the smile on her face until she reached her sister, Gwen. The captain bowed and moved away.

Jenny grabbed her sister's arm and pulled her behind a

potted plant so they were in relative privacy. "Please, Gwen, get me out of here! If I have to act stupid to satisfy the vanity of one more witless young man, I'll…I'll—"

"Scream?" suggested Gwen. She gave her twin a sympathetic smile, her bright blue eyes twinkling. "You might do better punching them in the eye, Jenny. I almost did."

Genevieve, the older of the twins, gave her sister a look of delight. "Who, Gwen? Was it Sir Gerald? He can be such a bore. Do you know he once gave me a jaw-me-dead when he caught me reading Plato in the original Greek? He actually told me ladies should not addle their brains with difficult reading materials. Their sole purpose in life is to look pretty so men can enjoy gazing upon them, act stupid so stupid men can feel intelligent, and faint at the sight of a spider so men can feel strong." She released a sound that was suspiciously like a snort—if ladies made such a sound, that is, which they didn't. Then she added darkly, "He did, however, think it was adorable that I was pretending to know how to read Greek."

Gwen giggled. "When were you reading Plato, Jenny?"

"Three days ago at Lady Jersey's rout. I was so tired of pretending to be something I'm not that I sneaked into the library for a good read. I was just getting to the good part when Sir Gerald walked in." She grimaced. "I was sorely tempted to draw his cork."

"Shh!" admonished Gwen. "If Mama hears you speaking cant she'll make us listen to a lecture about the proper behavior becoming a lady. I can't sit through another, I promise you. After the last one, I swore I'd run and hide."

"How very unladylike, Gwen, to be sure," replied her sister tartly. She spoiled the effect by laughing. Out of the corner of her eye, she saw the arrival of Lady Adam Prestwich. "Oh, let us go say hello to Bri, Gwen. I have not seen her this age. And she was always good for chasing away the doldrums."

The twin beauties moved sedately across the floor, smiling serenely at gentlemen as they went. Both were well versed in the art of flirtation and it was automatic for them to do so. If they weren't a duke's daughters with notoriously high dowries, they'd be considered on the shelf, in fact. They were three-and-twenty and both had been inundated with offers of marriage, still were, in fact. Neither had found gentlemen they liked well enough for marriage, however, and so they were both still unwed.

Upon reaching Lady Prestwich, Gwen burst out with, "Oh, Bri, you are the answer to our prayers." Then she caught sight of Miles Prestwich, a gentleman with whom she was slightly acquainted and more than slightly attracted to. She blushed prettily and offered him a smile.

Jenny noticed this little bit of by-play and rolled her eyes. Really, her sister could be such a ninny sometimes!

The sound of a male laugh jerked her attention to Bri's other escort. Her eyes widened considerably and she had to bite her lip to avoid embarrassing herself by laughing outright.

Before her stood a replica of Miles, only, somehow, much more handsome, but in a piratical sort of way. His hair was longer than fashion dictated and tied at his nape with a black silk ribbon. His evening dress was flawless, his cravat a miracle of starch and linen with a blue diamond glowing from the folds, and his dancing pumps shined like black glass.

He had a decidedly roguish look in his dark blue eyes. It was this look that made her think of pirates and made her want to laugh. He looked very out of place in the glittering ballroom surrounded by members of the *ton*.

He stared right back at her, his look frankly appraising and Jenny surprised herself by returning the look hundredfold. His eyes darkened and she felt goose flesh break out on her arms. Her heartbeat accelerated and her palms grew moist. And all that from a simple look! What would it be like to actually touch the man?

She became aware suddenly that everyone's attention was focused on her. "I'm sorry," she said. "I wasn't attending."

Bri laughed. "That was apparent, my dear. I was merely introducing Miles's brother, Dare. You may or may not acknowledge him, as is your preference," she said carelessly, grinning hugely. "He is a bit of a rogue, a bit of a flirt, and a bit of a rake." The older woman pursed her lips. "On second thought, you might do better to stay away from him."

Dare seemed much amused by this assessment of his character. He made no reply, however, beyond admonishing Bri to be careful whom she informed of this fact.

"You admit to being these things?" Jenny asked with raised eyebrows.

"I admit nothing, Lady Genevieve," he replied. "Confession leads too often to misunderstandings and assumptions better left...unassumed."

"Many would disagree, Mr. Prestwich, and say that confession more often leads to better understanding."

He snapped a smart bow, his eyes crinkling in amusement. "*Touché*, my dear lady."

The band chose that moment to strike up a waltz. Dare bowed to Jenny and asked if she cared to dance.

She accepted out of curiosity. "I was under the impression that you have been away for many years, sir. How is it that you know how to waltz?"

"What a savage you must think me," he remarked lightly, placing one hand at her waist while the other took her hand in a strong clasp. "I have not been among only the uncivilized, you know. The waltz is danced in Germany."

"I know that," she replied with a tinge of asperity. Did he actually believe her to be so stupid that she did not know in which country the waltz originated?

Dare grinned down at the diminutive beauty in his arms. "Indeed? You didn't exactly strike me as the type to know much beyond how to flirt and spend money."

He made the comment just to rile her and he got just the reaction he wanted. She puckered up like an angry kitten and he strongly suspected she'd hiss and spit at him if she could do so without destroying her reputation beyond any sort of atonement.

"I'll have you know," she said angrily before she thought about what she was saying and to whom, "I happen to read extensively on every subject I can get my hands on. I would wager I have read more than you."

"I would not take you up on that, little trumpeter," he commented dryly, "considering I avoid reading like the plague." Lord, he'd no idea the chit was a bluestocking. No wonder she was still unmarried at her advanced age.

As if she had read his mind, she said haughtily, "I do not go about bragging about my knowledge, sir. I know how to act around gentlemen."

"From that comment, I can deduce one of two things," he replied with a mocking twist of his finely molded lips. "One, you are a consummate actress and an accomplished liar or, two, you do not think me a gentleman and therefore subject me to your childish displays of temper and behavior."

Her mouth dropped open further and further with every word until he was sure she would catch flies were she not careful.

"How dare you, sir!" she finally responded scathingly. She attempted to stop dancing but he tightened his hold on her, lessening the distance between them to a mere few inches.

"Release me! This dance is over," she hissed.

"I think not, my dear. You were asking for that. I'll not let you insult me by leaving me alone on the dance floor."

So Jenny fumed silently until the dance was finished.

She refused to answer any of his questions or rise to any of his baiting. The dance finally ended and she was escorted back to her sister.

Dare bowed mockingly. "Thank you, my lady, for the dance. Rarely have I been so…entertained." He turned on his heel and walked away.

"Whatever did he mean by that?" wondered Gwen aloud.

"Oh, I don't know," snapped her sister, very annoyed indeed. "He is insufferable. I do not wish to speak about it."

Gwen obliged her by remaining silent. But she couldn't help but wonder what Darius Prestwich had said to so vex her twin.

"You were unforgivably rude to her, I think," Miles told his brother on the way home that night.

Dare grunted, refusing to answer. That girl had managed to annoy him in a way no lady had ever done before and he would not acknowledge that perhaps he'd been just a bit too hard on her.

"She is a spoiled brat, Miles. It was time she had a proper setdown."

Miles bristled. "She is a lady, Dare, not some strumpet who is paid to ignore your cruelty." He flushed suddenly and glanced at Bri's smirking face. "Your pardon."

Bri nodded and would have replied but Dare was not finished arguing his case.

"The differences between a strumpet and a lady are money and power, Miles. Otherwise, a woman is a woman and they are all alike." He sent Lady Prestwich a challenging look as if daring her to dispute his claim.

Bri just laughed. "For the most part, I have to agree. Oh, close your mouth, Miles, do before you catch a fly. As I was saying, ladies are not very different. Those without name merely sell their bodies in order to buy food. Ladies, on the other hand, sell their bodies into wedlock for position, security, and power. I leave it to you to determine the bigger whore of the two types."

Dare and Miles stared. Bri shrugged. "It's true, but I think Miles is right, Dare. Jenny is not deserving of your scorn, no matter what she said to you. If she were like other ladies, she'd have accepted the Duke of Bedford when he offered for her in her first season."

"Bedford offered for Lady Genevieve?"

Bri smiled at the gentlemen. "Yes. Now I think we should focus on something else. My gossiping went rather well, I think. Soon everyone will believe Rory and I helped Merri kill her husband." She was referring to her cousin's wife, Aurora, and their friend, Leandra, whose husband, the Duke of Derringer, had recently gone missing. This was what had taken Adam away unexpectedly and he had taken Aurora's husband, the Earl of Greville, with him.

Miles and Dare looked at her in disbelief and she laughed at the twin expressions. "It is when I say something so totally outrageous that the two of you actually look alike. Otherwise," she shrugged, "you are very easy to tell apart."

"I've never had any trouble," quipped Dare.

"Nor I," agreed Miles in a rare display of levity.

Dare gave him an approving look. "I knew I'd wear you down eventually," he remarked lightly.

Miles frowned. "One light comment does not mean I am just like you now, Dare."

"Heaven forbid! I wouldn't ever assume such a thing, brother. I realize what a sad trial I am to you and all others forced to endure my company. Please accept my most humble apologies." His look was a mask of humble penitence, eyes cast upward with a beseeching look and hands clasped before him as if in prayer.

"Oh, Dare," laughed Bri, "you are a delight. I envision

many interesting evenings this Season."

Three

Dare glared at his new gentleman's gentleman. The man insisted Dare have his hair cut and he was having none of it. After a heated debate regarding what was fashionable and what was not, Dare finally snapped.

"Shut your trap, you miserable fop!" he shouted. "I will not cut my hair, I will not change my attitude, and I will not bow to the whims of a starched-up tailor's dummy!"

"I never—!" began the man in righteous indignation.

"Well, perhaps you should!" snapped Dare. He growled low in his throat, a sound that was so like an animal the valet stared at him, his pupils dilated instinctively in fear.

"Get out," commanded Dare in a quieter voice. "I will hire someone willing to work with me, not against me."

The valet, upset at losing a job but grateful for his freedom nonetheless, fled before Dare could change his mind. Dare glared at the closed door and sighed. Lord, he couldn't do this. Moving about in the upper echelons of Society was wearing his patience dangerously thin.

He shoved a hand through his hair and stared at his reflection in the long mirror in his dressing room. His own face stared back, wavy black hair loose about his shoulders, his features set in lines of weariness. He didn't think he looked anything like Miles at the moment and that pleased him to no end. His entire life, he'd had to watch his twin charm their parents and do everything right. He graduated first in their class from Eton and then Miles had gone on to graduate first in his class at Cambridge while Dare had run away from home. Miles solved every problem their father came up against on the tiny estate they'd grown up on— Miles was perfect.

This is what he'd had to grow up with. A perfect mirror image of himself doing everything right, never playing pranks, never getting into trouble, never becoming a by-word in Society, never doing anything to sully his sterling character. Therefore, every little bit of trouble Dare had managed to land himself in looked ten times worse. Miles was held up as the ideal although Dare was technically older. When Dare had turned sixteen, he'd begged Adam to send him on one of his ships so he could get out from under the disapproving stares of his family.

He would be forever grateful to Adam for doing just that. His life at sea had been hard work and made him take life seriously for once. He had thrived under the strict supervision of Captain James Ford, a man who became more of a father to Dare than his own had been.

A sad little frown tipped Dare's lips as he thought of that gallant man. He had been aboard one of the ships that had been lost at sea. The *Aphrodite* had been the first to go down leaving the bodies of nearly every crewman floating in the water.

A chill ran over Dare every time he thought about it. He had been assigned to that ship but something had occurred to keep him bound to shore and he'd had to wait for the next of Adam's shipping line. His extended visit in France had not been pleasant but, considering the alternative, he was grateful for small favors.

"Problems?" inquired Miles from the door.

Dare didn't turn. "Nothing I need help with."

Miles entered the room, closing the door firmly behind him. "Why did you come back?" he asked bluntly.

Dare turned to regard his brother, his eyes carefully blank. "I wanted to reunite with my dear brother, of course," he said with a tinge of sarcasm. "Why do you think I returned?"

"To cause trouble," Miles snapped, his face a mask of well-bred calm and ease in spite of his hurtful remark.

Dare had the urge to destroy his brother's poise. Mostly because he envied him. Miles had always been held up as perfect. It was inevitable that Dare would believe it, too. That he wasn't a paragon as well had always been an open wound with him.

Dare assumed an air of surprise. "Trouble, brother? I never *cause* trouble. It just seems to follow me wherever I go. I'm hurt you'd think so poorly of me."

"Perhaps you can take it elsewhere this time," Miles suggested mildly.

"No," his brother stated bluntly, no longer jesting.

Miles sighed, shoving his hand through his short dark hair. "Why must you forever plague me?" he complained. "I thought you had found what made you happy and I was glad. I thought you'd not bother to come back with your... *trouble*. Why did you choose now?"

Dare stared at his twin. It was the closest Miles had ever come to outright saying he did not like him and would rather live without him around. He wondered if his brother's attitude had anything to do with a certain blue-eyed princess named Guinevere.

"What are you afraid of, Miles?" he asked gently. "Are

you still angry with me over Belinda?"

Belinda Markwell had been a neighbor of theirs growing up in Exeter. Miles had had a boyhood *tendre* on her since they were in shortcoats and Dare, in one of his stupider moments, seduced the girl just to spite Miles. It was not something he was proud of but it had happened and he firmly believed the past was better left in the past. Dwelling on it just led to hard feelings and heartache.

A small voice in his head told Dare he was a hypocrite in this particular belief but he ignored it.

Miles drew himself up, his blue eyes glinting angrily. "I will not talk about that, Dare. Belinda was a gently reared girl and you were despicable to use her in such a fashion."

"I know, Miles, I know." Dare sighed. "I apologized a thousand times over for that and I don't think I deserve to be reminded of my adolescent stupidity every day for the rest of my life."

"She's dead, Dare. You wouldn't marry her and she killed herself."

Dare froze. "You think that was my fault?" he asked.

"Everyone *knows* it was your fault. She was pregnant, Dare."

He hadn't known at the time. It wasn't until much later

that the truth had finally come out. But he also hadn't been the first or last man she'd been with. The possibility of the child being his was small.

He could have told Miles this and retained at least a tiny portion of his twin's respect. But he didn't want to harm Belinda's reputation any more than he already had. If everyone believed him to have abandoned her so callously, so be it. He could withstand the taint to his name. He didn't enjoy being in Society anyway.

An image of Genevieve Northwicke danced before his eyes. She was the daughter of the Duke of Denbigh. Why on earth had he thought of her at this inopportune moment?

Most likely because the young lady had affected him as no other woman he'd ever met, he admitted ruefully. He firmly pushed the memory of her appreciative stare from his mind. If he allowed himself to think of it now, he'd be in some considerable physical discomfort.

"I can see, as usual, that it is pointless trying to reason with you," muttered Miles in disgust. "I'll leave you to your fuming."

Dare said nothing. What could he say? Part of him agreed with his brother. The other was too proud to try to defend himself. Miles was his twin, his other half. Miles should have believed in him, trusted him.

But he didn't. Miles never had. No one ever had. Dare was very much afraid no one ever would.

Slumping down into a chair, Dare dropped his head into his hands, the picture of weary dejection. He suddenly wished he had stayed on that boat and returned to France.

That afternoon was spent in the traditional manner. Gentlemen who had stood up with ladies the night before paid a social call or sent round their card with flowers. Dare had to obey this social edict as well and he did so with calm indifference. Miles insisted on personally calling on Denbigh's twins and begged Dare to accompany him.

Dare envied his brother's ability to pretend their heated argument had not occurred. Evidently, he had run it through his mind and come up with a solution for it. Oh, well.

After laboriously dressing himself in one of the monkey suits he hated, Dare left his room to find his brother. Miles was in his own chamber, staring at his reflection in the mirror, clearly fretting over the folds of his cravat.

"You look well, Miles," Dare commented lazily. He sat down, slouching horribly, and gave his twin a flashing grin.

"How many more hours until you're ready?"

Miles swung around and looked his brother over critically. Dare was wearing a morning coat of dark blue bath superfine and skintight pantaloons gray-blue in color. On his feet were shining black Hessians. His cravat was nothing remarkable but nothing to be ashamed of either and had a sapphire stickpin inserted haphazardly in the folds. His wavy black locks were tied securely at his nape.

"You look very well, too," Miles finally said.

"I'm relieved my appearance pleases you, Miles," replied Dare dryly. "Can we go now? I'd like to get this visit over with if you don't mind."

Miles frowned at him. "I'll be down in a trice."

Dare stood with fluid grace and sauntered to the door. "I'll await you in the drawing room."

Upon reaching that room, however, Dare heard the unmistakable sounds of Bri receiving her own gentlemen callers from the evening before. He hesitated a second too long, debating whether or not to interrupt, and was accosted in the hall by a blond gentleman who reminded him sharply of Lady Genevieve.

This gentleman stopped and opened his mouth on his way down the stairs. Then he closed his mouth and peered closer. A smile broke out over his features. "You must be

Darius Prestwich."

"You have the advantage over me, I'm afraid," Dare replied easily. He was unsure what to make of this man who was obviously a relative of the Northwicke twins.

He stuck out a hand, looking up a little at Dare, as Dare stood a bit taller. "I am Adam's closest friend, Connor Northwicke."

Dare shook hands with Lady Genevieve's older brother. "And how is your wife?" Dare inquired politely. He had heard a few vague things about this gentleman from some of Adam's correspondence over the past few years and he privately thought Lord Connor had been through more than any man deserved.

His smile wavered. "She is well, thank you." He glanced away, his smile finally fading, and glanced back at Dare. "My sister mentioned you when I saw her today," he finally commented lightly.

Dare braced himself for what ever the little minx had happened to mention. "In what way?" he asked, keeping any shred of emotion from his tone.

"She seemed to think you said or did something to upset Jenny, actually. She said it wasn't important, just odd."

A little like this conversation, thought Dare. He forced

a look of vague interest and repeated his earlier question.

Lord Connor sighed a little. "I hate to do this to you since we just met but as Jenny's older brother I feel the need to warn you away from my sister." Dare stiffened, saying nothing. Connor continued, "Gwen seems to think Jenny's odd reaction stemmed from her partiality for you more than her disgust. I realize you are Adam's cousin and as such entitled to some courtesy. But your past is too shady by half." He paused, studying Dare's closed expression. "Damn. You know, there is really no graceful way to warn somebody off, is there?"

"Don't bother, Lord Connor. I understand completely and think more of you as a man to get involved in the future happiness of your sister. You have my solemn promise that after today, I will never speak to your sister again. And for good measure, I will include her twin in that promise."

"You do not have to do anything so drastic, Mr. Prestwich," Connor protested.

"I insist, my lord. Now, if you will excuse me, I must pay my compliments to my cousin." Dare strode into the drawing room, refusing to acknowledge the pain caused by Lord Connor's very negative assumption.

It was rather unfortunate for quite a few people that Dare's reckless streak was coming to the surface again, brought on by his own disappointment in himself and aided by certain comments and references to his past. But he was no more able to stop it than capture a wave in the palm of his hand.

Four

Bri looked up from her circle of admirers when Dare approached. "Dare, how lovely of you to join me. Will you sit?"

Dare bowed over her hand, smiling flirtatiously. "I regret that I cannot, my lady," he replied, straightening. "Miles and I must perform duty visits this afternoon."

Bri stared at him for a moment. Then, rising, she said, "I wonder if you might walk in the garden with me for just a moment, Dare. There is something I wish to discuss with you."

They were soon strolling amongst thorny roses and twisting vines of ivy. Both were silent for a moment, just gazing about at the signs of an early spring.

"Did you meet Con?" asked Bri suddenly, turning a blinding smile on her companion.

Dare stiffened slightly. "Lord Connor? I did. He was all that was… um, protective."

Bri gave him a sympathetic look. "That bad, huh?"

"Something like that."

Bri stopped, causing Dare to stop right along with her. She turned to look him in the eye. "I realize Connor means well, Dare, but please don't take anything he says personally. He is very protective of his sisters; they have always been extremely close."

"That is a difficult request, Bri," he remarked dryly. Her answering look was eloquent enough to make him laugh. "Why, you ask? Well, he referred to my past and that is something I can't help but take personally since it is something I have that no one else does."

"Nonsense," scoffed Bri. "Everyone has a past."

Dare was very quiet for a long moment. "Do you know anything about my past, Bri? Has Adam or Miles told you anything?"

"No," she admitted. "But it can't possibly be as bad as mine, Dare. No one has a past as bad as mine." Her tone was sad with a touch of bitterness and Dare wondered what she had hidden in her past to cause such an emotion.

"Not even Derringer?" he asked facetiously, having heard by now all about the infamous Lord Heartless.

She grinned. "Well, maybe Derringer," she conceded.

Dare sighed suddenly, a sigh of pure, unadulterated weariness. "I appreciate your attempt to cheer me, Bri, really I do. But it is unnecessary, as I had never once considered courting Lady Genevieve. She is a duke's daughter and I am merely the son of a country gentleman, owning nothing more than a scandalous past."

Bri gave him an enigmatic look. "Somehow I don't believe you are *merely* anything, Darius Prestwich."

Jenny and Gwen flirted with their visitors as they had been taught. A shy but inviting look here, a whispered word or two there, blushes and hand squeezes for good measure; these were the key ingredients for an experienced flirt.

The twins, however, had been entertaining gentlemen for the past few hours and their rather limited store of patience was wearing thin indeed. Jenny had already threatened to pop one young man in the nose if he insisted on treating her like she was without a brain, much to his astonishment. He had been so surprised, in fact, that he had convinced himself he had not heard her correctly and taken his leave in a state of semi-unreality.

Gwen, who actually possessed a bit more patience than her sister, finally got to the point that she was also ready to do someone serious bodily injury. That was when Darius and Miles Prestwich were announced. She smiled at Jenny, whose unpleasant scowl marred the perfection of her lovely features.

The new arrivals crossed the room, bowing and saying all that was expected of them, offering little clusters of flowers to each of the ladies. Gwen accepted hers from Miles with a maidenly blush and invited him to sit with her. Jenny accepted Dare's offering with a distinct lack of thankfulness and carelessly gestured at the chair next to her.

"Please sit, Mr. Prestwich," she said in a tone that indicated how clearly she did not wish him to sit there.

"Always willing to oblige a lady," murmured Dare, already amused by his rude reception.

Jenny snorted. "Indeed? You shock me, sir."

"Not nearly so much as I could," Dare pronounced with a certain amount of wicked innuendo. Her look informed him that his dart was well aimed.

"How is your day progressing, Lady Genevieve?" he asked politely.

"Oh, you know, as usual," she replied with a ludicrous expression of boredom on her face. "I flirt, I flatter, I charm, I choke."

Dare laughed, drawing the attention of some of the other gentlemen in the room, as well as the ladies. He appeared completely unaware of this, however. "You are just as candid as ever, my lady," he told her. He sobered suddenly. "Don't ever lose that. Act the débutante to the hilt if you must but never marry until you find someone with whom you can be yourself."

Jenny stared at him. "Does such a man exist?" she asked with a small amount of wonder.

"Of course. I wouldn't think your brother ever found much pleasure in talking to stupid ladies and I can't imagine that his wife is like that. You know Bri is outspoken and Adam seems to delight in that. Even Miles believes women should have some brains and he seems to take Society's side in everything."

"And what about you?" Jenny heard herself ask, vastly interested in this topic and curious about the hint of bitterness she detected in his words.

His face became shuttered, distant. "I much prefer stupid ladies," he remarked in a tone devoid of expression. He stood. "Please excuse me, my lady." He bowed and left her to join a group of young men standing near the window overlooking the street.

If that was what he liked, why was he counseling her to retain her independence of mind? It made no sense to her and even less the more she thought about it. When the middle-aged Earl of Tarence joined her, she smiled and became as distant as Dare had been towards her.

"I can't believe you would make other plans, Dare. Adam wanted you and I to take Bri and Lady Greville about," complained Miles that evening.

"I'm sure you can handle it, Miles," he said encouragingly. "I believe in you."

"You say that now. But Lady Greville is six months pregnant and scary beyond reason. And I think Bri is, too. She just hasn't told anyone yet."

"She is. About three months, I should think."

"You see? I need support, Dare. Me, alone with two pregnant females? The mind shudders."

Dare's lips became a grim line as he studied Miles. "When the devil did you turn into such a whiner?"

Miles drew himself up to his full height of six-feet-one-inch. If he did it to intimidate him, Dare thought, he was in for a disappointment. Darius Prestwich was not easily intimidated—especially by his younger brother.

"I do not whine, Dare. I have legitimate concerns. I choose to voice these concerns. And since they are about you, who better to listen to them?"

Dare stared up at him from where he lounged in his chair. His expression was patronizing. "Miles, when will you learn? I do not listen to anyone. I am my own man. A violent, irresponsible, and sometimes downright nasty man, true, but my own man nonetheless. Please refrain from telling me what I should and should not do." He stood, patting Miles's cheek affectionately. "Thank you, brother. I'll see you tomorrow."

Miles escorted Bri and Aurora, Lady Greville, to a rout in Park Lane being held by Sir Alfred Tinney and his new bride, Lady Matilda. With a lady on each arm, Miles led them up the front steps and the three of them greeted their host and hostess. They fought their way up the stairs to the upper salons. Miles relinquished his charges to some of their acquaintances so they could further their gossip about Lord Derringer and escaped to a slightly less crowded room.

He had stood looking around the room for only a few moments when he caught sight of the Ladies Northwicke. They held court from a settee situated near a potted palm.

He moved in that direction.

Gwen greeted him with obvious pleasure. This was what a young lady ought to be like. She was polite, sweet, unassuming, kind, beautiful, elegant... he could go on forever.

Jenny looked up at him with a question in her eyes that Miles couldn't begin to understand. He glanced at Gwen, his black brows raised ever so slightly.

Lady Guinevere rose to her feet. "I would very much like to walk a bit, Mr. Prestwich," she said sweetly.

Miles bowed and offered his arm. He sent a questioning glance Jenny's way but she politely refused to accompany them.

When they were a sufficient distance away, he remarked, "Your sister seemed to want to ask me something."

"I believe she wonders where your brother is, sir," she told him.

"But why would she want to know that? I thought they took a dislike to each other."

His companion smiled enchantingly. "Have you not heard that there is a thin line between love and hate, sir? I do believe my sister reacts so to your brother because she is enamored of him. I have never seen her react so to another man, I assure you."

"Perhaps I should warn her about him," murmured Miles thoughtfully, glancing back at Denbigh's other daughter.

"Oh, please do not, Mr. Prestwich," said Gwen in distress. "I should not have spoken so out of turn, you see. It would embarrass her greatly to discover she had been found out. I regret telling my brother about it but I cannot undo that now."

"Lord Connor is aware of their attraction?" he asked in disbelief. He hoped the other man had refrained from mentioning it to Dare. If Dare was warned off, he might court the girl just to spite everyone.

"Yes, I am afraid so. I confessed in a moment of unease over the angry words they exchanged yesternight. Con assured me he would look into it. I only hope he didn't find anything…alarming."

Miles nearly groaned aloud. Of course, Lord Connor found something alarming lurking in Dare's past. And Dare had mentioned meeting Lord Connor earlier that very day. It was inevitable that Lord Connor warned Dare to stay away from his sister.

"Mr. Prestwich? Miles? Whatever is the matter?"

The distress in Gwen's soft voice pierced his

ruminations and he smiled down at the petite beauty. "You just called me Miles," he said in some wonder.

"I admit, I did," she confessed, her face turning a becoming shade of pink. "I apologize if you thought it forward of me, sir, but I could not get your attention otherwise."

"I do not think it forward of you, my lady. I would be honored if you would call me Miles. And," he added with a special smile that warmed her to her toes, "you always have my attention."

Five

He tried, he really did. But it was no use. Dare's contrary nature would not be silenced. He had been told a few things about Lord Connor that made him uneasy but he was self-destructive enough to disregard his own common sense. He decided to try to woo Lady Genevieve just to prove he could.

He had no way of knowing that Lady Genevieve, who had been hurt at his obvious defection, was just as determined to ignore him should he try to come around now. Although, after a lecture from her brother, she was just as tempted to flout convention.

Jenny was crossing the hall to enter the library when Connor stepped into the foyer. She went down to greet him with a hug and kiss, as was her habit, and inquired after his wife and children.

"They are well, Jenny, they are well," he said, smiling. "I wonder, could you spare me a few moments? I'd like to talk to you."

"You came expressly to see me?" she asked in some surprise.

"Do not sound so like I ignore you the rest of the time, Jenny, I beg you. You make me feel like a boor," he complained good-naturedly.

"You could never be that, Con," she said. "I was just on my way to the library to see if Father has a book on phosphates. I heard about this new way of planting that has me itching to read more about it but I also want to compare it to other writings about the use of phosphates."

Connor smiled at her enthusiasm for a topic most ladies shuddered to even think about. "I could share a bit of my own knowledge on the subject but I have a lowering feeling that you already know more than I do."

"Perhaps," she allowed. "But we could talk about it anyway."

Connor took her arm and led her into their father's spacious library. He steered her to a set of chairs flanking the large fireplace and pushed her down into one of them. His face was serious, intent, as if he had some dreadful news to impart.

"Con, please tell me what is bothering you," she implored. "You are scaring me with your long face. Verena and the children are all well?"

"Yes, I said already they are, Jenny," he responded. He sat down in the chair opposite and leaned forward, settling his elbows on his knees. "I wonder if you'd tell me how you feel about Darius Prestwich."

Her blond brows shot up. "Darius Prestwich?" she repeated numbly. "I find him insufferable, if you must know."

Her brother drew a deep breath. "You have no tender feelings for the man?" he insisted.

"None, Con. What is this about?" Her tone bordered on exasperation as she watched the consternation settle on Connor's face.

"I was told you were partial to him, is all. Apparently, my source was wrong."

"Who is this source, Con?" she asked with dangerous softness.

He looked at her shrewdly. "My own imagination, Jenny." He rose to his feet, apparently ready to leave. "It appears my reason for coming was unnecessary. I wanted to ascertain your feelings for him because he apparently has feelings for you. But he shouldn't bother you now."

Jenny stared at him from her seat. "Now?"

"He promised to stay away from you. And I believe him. He did not seem too upset about it," he murmured reflectively. "Relieved, in fact."

With a brother's usual carelessness, Connor managed to severely wound Jenny's *amour propre*. "What do you mean, he seemed *relieved*?"

"Don't take it to heart, Jen. Darius is not interested in you because he is not interested in marriage. A man of his stamp is only interested in one thing. And he can't get that from a gently bred female."

Jenny wasn't naïve enough to misunderstand her brother's explanation. But she was still upset that Darius seemed to have no interest in her at all. Even an improper one would be a salve to her vanity.

Connor took his leave and his sister bid him a rather absentminded goodbye, her thoughts elsewhere. The words of her brother were burned into her mind, making her angrier by the second. She'd show them, she thought with grim determination. She'd show them both.

Dare eyed his cousin's wife with a certain amount of dislike. She certainly was an annoyingly persistent woman, he thought for the thousandth time. He didn't know why she seemed to think he had to escort her. Miles was a perfectly capable escort and Dare had no stomach for the opera. The mere thought of sitting through hours of caterwauling made him shudder.

"I won't go, Bri," he told her firmly. "You have Miles. I am unnecessary."

"You don't understand," she protested. "Connor's sisters, the daughters of the Duke of Denbigh, asked for you and Miles personally. It is an honor that you cannot decline."

"Let somebody else have the honor," snapped Dare. He was through arguing about it.

"Dare," Bri said then in a conciliating tone, "I would greatly appreciate it if you would come along. I love your brother, but even you have to admit, Miles is a bit of a dull old stick."

Dare unwillingly released a bark of laughter. "I do agree. But I promised to stay away from Denbigh's daughters, Bri. I mean to try to keep that promise."

"Oh, that," murmured Bri, remembering the conversation they'd had earlier that week. "This hardly counts," she dismissed. "You are obviously being dragged to the opera. Anyone with eyes will be able to see that you would rather be anywhere else. Connor will not cause a scandal by calling you out over your attendance even if we do sit with his sisters."

Dare crossed his arms over his chest and stared at her for a long moment. Then he gave a resigned sigh, saying, "Very well, Bri. You win. I'll go. Just give me a moment to dress."

Dare disappeared to his rooms and seriously considered dressing like a pirate, complete with black eyepatch. The Opera Committee was known for being nearly as strict as Almack's and he knew if he dared show up in such scandalously casual garb, he'd be tossed out on his ear.

He threw on his clothes unmindful of the way they landed on himself, and tied his cravat in something that looked remarkably well considering he hated the things and avoided them whenever possible. He pushed his hand instead of a comb through his black curls, crammed a hat on his head, shrugged into his coat of black superfine, shoved his feet into shiny black shoes, and walked out the door.

Bri took one look at him and smiled warmly. "You look very handsome, Dare."

Dare's eyes narrowed. "Why? Did I forget my breeches? Is my hat backwards? Shoes on the wrong feet? What is it?" His eyes crinkled with unholy amusement.

"Perhaps I should fetch my eyepatch?"

"No, you wretched man, no. We will depart now. Miles, come along," ordered Bri firmly. Then, with a gentleman on each arm, she left.

Jenny waited impatiently for Bri's party to arrive. She sat in the back of their box at the opera and scanned the crowded house in case they had decided to sit somewhere else. She was anxious to put her plan into action and she didn't mean to lose a single opportunity.

Her sister sat beside her, watching her with concern. "Jenny, you look flushed. Are you feeling quite the thing? Perhaps we should go."

Jenny gave her an impatient glance. "I am feeling fine. And you know how Mama loves the opera, Gwen. We couldn't leave now if Napoleon escaped again and threatened to murder anyone who refused to leave."

"Oh, don't say such things, Jenny! That man was horrible. And isn't he dead anyway?"

"I don't know, Gwen," she snapped. "Now, do be quiet. I'm looking for someone."

Gwen's eyes widened making them appear bluer and

more vibrant than usual. "You are? Who on earth—"

They arrived at that moment, cutting off Gwen's question. Jenny blushed hotly as she turned and her eyes collided with those of Darius Prestwich. His held amusement and a determination that Jenny did not understand.

He approached her after greeting her mother and father, the Duke and Duchess of Denbigh. She saw her father give him an intent look and prayed he'd not say anything embarrassing. Her mother was everything that was gracious and kind. Bri and Lady Greville were soon sitting next to the ducal pair, chatting happily until the start of the opera.

Dare and Miles moved to pay their respects to the twins. Their dark heads bent over the hands of the Denbigh twins made a stunning contrast that was not lost upon several audience members. Whispers started in one corner and soon spread throughout the building.

After seating themselves, each beside the lady of his choice, Dare turned to Jenny and said, "May I say how lovely you are this evening?"

"Certainly," she replied, fluttering her eyelashes in an exaggerated fashion. "I do so love compliments."

Dare smiled slightly. "Indeed? You seem to have

forgotten to whom you speak."

"Why do you say that, sir?"

"It's me, Jenny. Dare. You do not have to play the empty-headed twit with me."

Her expression became something ludicrous in its dismay. "Oh, dear. And I seem to recall you telling me you like stupid women."

His eyes glinted mischievously. "Are you trying to attract my attention, Jenny-love?"

She gave him an arch look, her insides quivering at the unexpected endearment. "How do I answer that, Mr. Prestwich? If I say yes, I must be fast. And if I say no, I am just rude."

"What are you two whispering about?" Miles queried suspiciously.

Jenny gave him her brightest smile. "Just trifling things, I assure you, Miles. Your brother has been delighting me with his wit."

"Indeed?" Miles murmured, giving his twin a searching glance.

Dare grinned. "Yes, Miles, my wit. I have been known to have one or two upon occasion."

Jenny stifled a giggle behind her fan. Her mother turned an admonitory glare on her, as the music was about to start. Placing an expression of utmost innocence on her pretty face, Jenny stared at the stage. Her lips quirked when she felt Dare's dark blue eyes on her.

She rapped him across the knuckles with her fan. "Stop staring, sir, it's rude."

"Rude?" he whispered. "In what way? I am merely enjoying the view."

"Watch the stage, Darius Prestwich," she ordered, blushing in spite of her determination to remain impassive and in control.

"I'd much rather watch you," he murmured, daringly taking her hand.

"I do believe you are flirting with me," she told him with a tiny smile tipping the corners of her mouth.

"And if I am?" he challenged, stroking his thumb over her palm.

Mesmerized by the patterns he was creating in her palm, Jenny had to still the sudden beating of her heart and the shiver of excitement that skittered along her spine. Visions of his hand doing more than caressing her gloved fingers stopped her lungs from drawing air.

She stuttered a bit before she could discernibly reply. Then, "I would not stop you," she said boldly.

The duchess turned and shushed them, causing the

duke to turn as well and give Dare a long look. Dare unobtrusively released his companion's hand and smiled at her father. The duke did not return the look. He just swiveled back to face the stage.

Dare leaned toward his fair companion, saying in a reverent voice, "I do believe your parents actually *listen* to the music." His expression was suitably horrified.

"They are quite unfashionable that way," she murmured back, tossing a careless smile at Miles, who was trying to hear what they were saying. "I should think your dear brother would be better off listening to the music as well."

"I shall call the blackguard out, I promise you, if he persists in starring at us. Does he give us the evil eye, do you think?"

Jenny giggled, only to cut it short when her father again turned with a stern expression on his face. She sent him an innocent grin and shushed Dare for good measure.

Dare and Jenny said nothing more for the rest of the performance. Neither was inclined to draw any more attention.

Six

Dare made sure to see much of Jenny over the coming days. She seemed as determined to see him. They managed to avoid Lord Connor's discerning eye since he was preoccupied with his own family. They would have been surprised to note that the duke was ever watchful, and usually with more insight into the situation than one would have ever thought.

Bri was a willing accomplice in many of Dare's encounters with the lovely Lady Genevieve. She often invited the delightful twin ladies to tea, gossiping and sharing fashion secrets.

Dare knew Bri didn't really like talking about fashion and had an almost violent dislike for gossip. He was secretly amused she was so transparently trying to bring him together with Jenny.

On the other hand, he wondered just what she was hoping to accomplish. While he was at it, he had to wonder just what he hoped to accomplish.

It was madness. And yet...

And yet, he knew he couldn't stop seeing her. Something in her called out to him, something unnamed, something...special.

"I have no honor," he muttered half to himself one day.

Jenny, having heard him, started. "Whatever do you mean?"

He favored her with a searching look. "I gave my word of honor that I would not see you."

Jenny just stared at him, her fingers gone suddenly numb around her delicate teacup. Moving with precision, she set the cup aside, careful not to jar it against the saucer or tabletop.

"Indeed? And to whom did you say such a thing?"

Her companion looked away, his gaze sweeping Bri's drawing room, seeing nothing and everything. Miles spoke quietly with Gwen and Bri, giving them a moment of privacy. The first footman stood in one corner, anticipating the needs of Bri's guests.

When his probing gaze again met hers, he had carefully masked his feelings. "Your brother, of course."

Jenny inwardly seethed. "Con interferes too much in my choice of companions, I think."

A smile of male satisfaction twisted his lips. "You care,

Jenny-love?"

She released a breath of air that sounded suspiciously like a snort. "You could only be so fortunate."

A moment of shared amusement passed. Then Jenny asked, hesitantly, not looking up from her tightly clasped hands, "Why do you continue to see me, sir? Does your honor mean nothing to you?"

Her eyes rose slowly, meeting his with an earnest desire for the truth and damn him, he wanted to tell her the truth.

He settled for a half-truth. "I find that your company means more to me than my honor," he told her simply, sincerely. He was a little unnerved that it was true.

Jenny's mind wandered as her maid dragged a brush through her golden locks. She should not read more into the statement than was warranted, she told herself sternly. It would only lead to heartache when he decided to entertain himself with more...worldly...company.

"Are you all right, my lady?"

Jenny met Alice's concerned gaze in the mirror. Brow furrowed, she asked why.

The maid looked confused herself. "You sighed as if you'd lost your dearest companion."

Jenny forced a smile to her stiff lips. "Did I? I was just missing Denbigh, Alice. No need to fret."

The maid appeared relieved it was something as simple as common homesickness that ailed her lady. Jenny wished bitterly that that was all it was.

The door to her chamber was pushed wide to admit Gwen, the Duchess of Denbigh following close behind.

Jenny rose to her feet, dismissing Alice with a nod of her head. She offered a sincerely pleased smile to her female family members.

Gwen grinned back but there was a stiff quality to it that made Jenny uneasy.

The duchess closed the door carefully behind her. She stood for a moment, facing the wooden barrier. Jenny felt a stirring of unease deep in her stomach.

Lady Denbigh turned. Her timelessly beautiful face was determinedly blank, not a whit of her inner feelings coming to the fore. She moved with infinite grace to her daughter's side, her hands clasped before her.

Jenny wished she possessed a tiny bit of her mother's poise. She had always loved her mother and wanted to be *her* when she grew up. Now, seeing the disappointment slowly unfurl in her parent's beautiful blue eyes, she wished she were anywhere but there.

She cast her eyes to her twin, questioning her. Gwen's smile was strained and after a moment, faded completely.

"We are concerned for you, my love," the duchess said softly. She took her daughter's hands in a comforting clasp, squeezing gently. "You have been spending much time at the Prestwich's residence."

"Gwen has visited too," Jenny offered, confused.

Her grace nodded. "Yes, dear, I know. What concerns me is your association with Mr. Darius Prestwich."

Jenny didn't say a word. She just looked at her mother, waiting.

Lady Denbigh sighed. With a little tug, she pulled her child over to the bed and sat down. Gwen joined them.

"If I ask you about your feelings for Mr. Prestwich, will you be honest, I wonder?"

Since it appeared to be a rhetorical question, Jenny said nothing.

"I am your mother, Genevieve, and I love you. I know you have very strong feelings for this young man and I'm not sure you understand exactly what it is about him that worries your brother."

"Con spends too much time with his nose in other

people's affairs," Jenny retorted bitterly.

"Perhaps," her mother allowed magnanimously. "But I think he has reason to be concerned, Jenny."

Jenny realized her mother would not leave it be until she'd revealed the cause of all the worry. So, with a heartfelt, bone-weary sigh, she invited, "Tell me what he's done, Mama."

Denbigh caught up with Dare one day on his way to Brooks's. The duke was driving his own team when he came upon the young man walking sedately.

"I say, Prestwich!" he called.

Dare turned a look of surprise on Jenny's father. "Your grace, how do?" he asked politely.

"Tolerably, tolerably," he replied, smiling. "Can I take you up, young sir?"

"That depends, in part, on where you are bound, Lord Denbigh."

"Anywhere you need to go."

Dare laughed. "Very well, then, sir. I am bound for my club," he said as he nimbly climbed up next to the older man.

Jaimey Grant

Denbigh set the team in motion and silence reined for a few minutes as he maneuvered the vehicle through some heavily trafficked areas. Shortly before they arrived at Dare's desired destination, Denbigh spoke.

"I understand you've been seeing much of my daughter, Mr. Prestwich."

Dare stiffened. "Yes, sir, I have."

"I also understand that her brother warned you to stay away from her."

"Yes, sir."

"Why, may I ask, do you disregard his warning?"

Dare gave his companion a rather pointed look. "If you believe there is any reason to warn me off, as I am sure you do, then you know me well enough to determine the answer to that question yourself."

A smile twisted the duke's lips briefly. "Indeed, I do, lad, indeed I do. I was just curious to hear what you would tell me."

"Now you have, your grace. And let me assure you that I am delighted to have been able to afford you some pleasure this day. You may let me down anywhere along here."

"Don't go puckering up, lad," admonished Denbigh. "I am not amused, actually, or pleased. I would like to

70

reiterate Connor's warning to you. My daughter is a lady, sir, and I will not have her trifled with. If you do not press toward marriage, I will ask that you desist pestering her."

"I sincerely mean your daughter no harm, Lord Denbigh," replied Dare wearily. "We are friends, nothing more. It seems I am the only man in Society with whom she can be herself. I am pleased to be able to give her that reassurance. I apologize for causing you or your family any unnecessary worry." He frowned. "I am not so simple that I do not realize she can do much better than me for a husband."

The duke pulled up before Brooks's Gentleman's Club. As Dare made to climb down, Denbigh said, "Remember those words, Darius Prestwich, every time you see Jenny. She deserves better."

Seven

At first, the duke's comments did not bother Dare. But as he contemplated them, he became more and more angry. So he had made one very stupid, careless mistake in his youth. Why must everyone hold it against him and make him feel as though he was not worth the dirt under their boots?

Dare was in an unpredictable mood by the time he returned home later that evening. He walked in the door to be informed that he was expected to escort Bri and Aurora by himself as Miles had come down suddenly with a cold. He nearly swore but something hard inside him made him tell Bri he would, of course, be delighted to escort her and her friend.

Bri actually shivered at the expression on his face when he said it.

When he reached his room, Dare stood before his mirror and stared at his reflection. Perhaps he should cut his hair, he thought dispassionately. He had had enough derogatory comments about it and he was about fed up with them. But he liked his hair. Perhaps he would give it some more thought before he did anything so drastic.

He spun away and marched across the room, entering his dressing room to change. Just as he shrugged out of his tight-fitting jacket and loose shirt, he heard a quiet scratching on his bedchamber door. With no thought for his half-naked state, he marched back across and threw the door open.

"What?" he barked, the unpredictability in his mood making itself known. He was never rude to servants.

Adam's butler, West, gave Dare a blank look and said solemnly, "This was delivered for you earlier, sir. I was informed to deliver it to you personally."

He handed over a small square of paper with no outstanding markings anywhere on it to indicate from whom it may have come. The seal was plain wax and of a color anyone could have. There were no smells attached to it and nothing written on it.

Dare took it with a curious look and asked, "Who delivered it?"

"A young boy, sir," replied the butler woodenly.

Dare stared at it a second longer, then, recalling the butler's presence, muttered, "Thank you, West," and shut the door in the man's face.

He took the note over to the window and sat down at the table situated there. Cracking the seal, he opened it and started to read. An incredulous expression settled on his countenance when he'd finished. He looked up and stared straight ahead for a few moments, not quite sure what to do. His dark blue eyes flashed back down at the feminine handwriting.

This was a coil, to be sure. Lady Genevieve could not have thought this through. What she was asking went against everything he believed and practiced as a gentleman.

He was positive she had told no one of her letter or intent, even her sister. He was also sure she would not. He wondered what drove the girl. Was she actually attracted to him or was she just after the proverbial forbidden fruit? If her family was diligent enough to warn him away from her, he knew they would warn her about him. Perhaps they'd even gone so far as to...

And why wouldn't they? Dare gave himself a shake. Of course, that was what the important thing was that she wanted to speak to him about. Her family must have told her about Belinda Markwell.

He stood up and stretched his arms far up over his

head. He would have had to tell her at some point, he thought in resignation. He just hoped she'd listen.

Two hours later Dare was bathed and fully dressed in dark jacket, tight silver breeches, silver waistcoat embroidered with gold thread, starched cravat tied just so with a black pearl stuck—in the usual haphazard fashion— through the folds, pristine white linen, and shiny black dancing shoes with silver buckles. He assessed his appearance critically in the long mirror and decided he would have to do. His hair was tied securely at his nape with a silver silk ribbon. He grinned suddenly, feeling an unusual tremor of excitement as he left the room.

"Dare! It's about time, you clunch," admonished Bri with a mock glare as soon as he entered the drawing room. "Well, at least you are ready at last." She grinned suddenly. "You look very well."

"As do you, Bri, as always," he returned, his eyes glowing with appreciation at the seductive appearance that she made in her clinging sapphire silk. "Adam is a very lucky man."

She thanked him, hurrying them out the door.

They were fashionably late for Lady Riesley's ball. Her daughter, Mirabel, was making her comeout and no expense had been spared. It was one of the premier events of the Season.

And Dare, with a thrum of excitement snaking through his veins, wished desperately that he were anywhere else.

He entered with his party, unobtrusively scanning the crowded ballroom for Lady Genevieve Northwicke. He spotted her on the dance floor, waltzing with some nonentity of a man.

An unaccountable stab of what felt suspiciously like jealousy speared him through the gut. It was all he could do to stay where he was and not go charging across the floor, intent on bodily harm.

Firmly restraining the impulse, he smiled a greeting to their hostess, who still stood in the receiving line although it was quite past time for her to join her guests. Her daughter had long since made her way into the ballroom on her father's arm, to open the dancing. He spotted the pretty young woman on the other side of the room, talking with great animation to the court of gentlemen surrounding her.

He responded vaguely to some comment made by Lady Riesley, offering a charming smile. She looked a little startled, as if he'd done something completely unexpected.

He glanced at his brother, whose mouth was set in grim lines.

Presently, they made their way into the crowd, exchanging greetings here and there, flirting gently and spreading yet more gossip on Lady Derringer's behalf.

Dare did it all without thinking. His mind was wholly taken up with trying not to look at Lady Genevieve and striving not to feel that insane jealousy again. She could dance with whomever she liked. He had no right to say otherwise.

Smiling pleasantly at a young lady he was sure he'd met but couldn't remember, he moved off to the edge of the room. He needed a moment alone with Jenny. He had to ask her what her aim was in writing him such a request as she had.

He stood where he knew she would end up when the dance ended. He ignored his brother, who had given him a puzzled look when Dare moved away from him. But then the appearance of Lady Guinevere snagged Miles's attention and he had no more time to wonder about his twin's actions.

The waltz duly ended, the gentlemen bowing, ladies curtsying. Jenny smiled charmingly at her handsome partner, whispering something Dare would have given his right arm to hear. Then, surprisingly, they made their way in his direction.

He straightened from his relaxed position from the column against which he leaned. He tried to gauge the mood of the lady but was stymied by the odd glint in her cornflower blue eyes.

"Mr. Prestwich," she said with a smile, her eyes lighting perceptibly.

Her companion favored Dare with an expression of distinct hostility. Dare grinned irrepressibly, ignored the man, and turned back to Jenny.

"Lady Genevieve, how enchanting you look this evening," he murmured, taking her hand. He leaned forward to kiss her hand, pausing and meeting her eyes just before he deftly turned it, pressing his lips to her gloved palm.

A delicious shiver snaked through her body and his smile grew decidedly wicked.

The gentleman at her side glared awfully at Dare, protesting, "Lady Genevieve, I must warn you against this fellow. Did you but know—"

"I know all I need to, my lord, and have had quite enough of warnings this eve." She smiled up at him, her eyes daring him to argue with a lady. "Thank you for your escort. I have promised this dance to Mr. Prestwich and I assure you, I am quite safe in his…capable…hands."

Dare almost snorted. He wondered if his bloody lordship had caught the slight hesitation in her words. If she had even an inkling of the kinds of thoughts he was currently entertaining about her, she'd run for cover…he hoped.

He allowed his gaze to wander over her generous curves again, pausing at the creamy expanse of bosom made visible by her low décolletage. The things he imagined doing to this particular young woman made his breath catch painfully in his throat.

Pale pink muslin twisted and flared, briefly revealing the curve of her hip. It was all Dare could do to keep his hands to himself. He wanted to touch her, fill his senses with her, devour her.

Damn. He had to get his thoughts under control.

"Mr. Prestwich?"

Dare started, making the mistake of meeting her gaze. Jenny's widened at what he assumed was untrammeled lust coloring his eyes. He saw a flaring of something similar in hers, an expression that shocked him. He felt an uncomfortable tightening in his groin and swiftly reined in his unruly reflections lest someone notice and start unwelcome talk.

And then Jenny giggled and Dare could hear the underlying hysteria. He realized she didn't really understand even a modicum of what she was feeling.

Oh, to be the man to teach her all about it. What an impossible dream, he mused in defeat.

"Lady Genevieve, your pardon. I was... woolgathering."

"Show a little respect, man," snapped the lord who, unaccountably, was still with them.

Dare gave him a lazy look from beneath half-lowered eyelids. "Are you still here?"

The man sputtered a moment in indignation. Jenny rescued the situation, placing a hand on the lord's arm. Dare wanted very badly to rip the man's arm off and take Jenny severely to task for daring to touch another man.

"Lord Grissom, I realize you only worry over my welfare, but I assure you, Mr. Prestwich will do me no harm." Her eyes met Dare's briefly, questioningly.

He smiled in as nonthreatening a manner as he could, considerably sure he resembled something quite feral. Lord Grissom bowed stiffly, firmly dismissed as he was by the lady present.

Dare took Jenny's hand, placing it on his arm. "Ah, my

beautiful damsel, I finally have you all to myself."

Jenny laughed lightly, casting an amused look around the crowded ballroom. "Hardly, my dear sir. Would that you did."

He stared at her. Had she truly said what he thought he heard? When she smiled, he knew he had and, amazingly, he was flummoxed.

"Have I finally managed to render you speechless, Darius Prestwich? I have to admit I am delighted."

He shook his head, trying for a semblance of reason, trying to ignore the sudden clamoring in his veins to take her somewhere, anywhere, and make her fully aware of what it was she so wantonly offered.

"Did I really solicit this dance?" he asked instead.

"Of course not. I was heartily sick of Grissom's tiresome lectures on proper behavior. As if he has room to talk," she grumbled. "The man has two mistresses that I know of whom he openly visits—they actually share a house—and I'm sure they are not the first."

Dare released a short bark of laughter. "Ah, but you miss the point, my dear girl. Gentlemen are *allowed* to have mistresses. Ladies are not allowed to even dally without severe consequences."

"How unfair is that?"

Dare groaned. "Jenny, my girl, don't wish for things that are better left unexplored. You are far too inquisitive for your own good."

She frowned up at him. "You begin to sound like Lord Grissom."

Grimacing, he began walking the edge of the room, keeping a careful eye out for her family, the male members especially. The last thing he wanted was a public scene.

"I have no intention of sounding like the prosy Lord Grissom, I assure you," he told her sincerely. "I just thought a word of caution necessary as you sounded quite like you actually wanted to be"—he searched for a word that was not terribly insulting—"fast."

"I don't. Want to be labeled fast, I mean. I just wish men were held up to ridicule the same as women. It's clearly unfair to condemn one for one's action simply because she had the misfortune to be born female while praising a man for hopping from bed to bed with not a care in the world for his family at home."

Dare gave her a long considering look. "I must say I agree, Lady Genevieve, but to actually say what you just did in such a public setting is courting censure."

Jenny spared a surreptitious glance for the assembled guests, noting a few within hearing were giving her queer looks. She sent them a beatific smile and turned back to her companion.

"It is no worry. Mrs. Garber is no gossip and Lord Woods only pretends he can hear. He is actually deaf as a post."

Dare chuckled. "Thankfully for your reputation, my dear."

"Yes." She paused a moment. Dare wondered what was going on in that fertile brain of hers but was patently afraid to ask. "Do you mind very much if we sit this dance out?" she finally inquired, turning innocent cornflower eyes up to his.

It was a second before he actually realized the orchestra had started the next dance. He smiled back at her, inclining his head ever so slightly and steering her in the direction of some empty chairs along the wall.

"Oh, do you think we could go out on the terrace? It is a bit stuffy in here."

"Certainly," he agreed, against his better judgment. He moved with her to the tall doors leading out into the rather chilly March night. He eyed her a bit skeptically. "Are you sure? There is a chill wind in the air."

Her answering smile should have warned him she was up to mischief. But part of him recalled that odd note she'd sent round earlier that night and he wanted to speak with her privately about it.

He led her out, staying carefully within sight of anyone who happened to look in their direction.

Jenny had other ideas, however.

"Oh, what a beautiful fountain! Let's take a closer look, shall we?" Holding out her hand for his arm, there was really nothing he could do but escort her halfway across the rather vast English garden to the misting fountain in the center.

It was really nothing extraordinary that he could tell, but Jenny seemed quite taken with the thing. He imagined it was supposed to represent Aphrodite or some such mythical goddess but the weather and time had eroded it down to something closely resembling a dyspeptic squirrel holding a water jug.

"Isn't it lovely. So romantic."

Alarm bells went off in his head. Lady Genevieve Northwicke couldn't possibly have dalliance in her inventive little mind...could she?

His question was answered about a second later. Turning slightly, she stretched up and placed her lips firmly against his.

Eight

He wasn't doing anything, she thought in sudden panic. Jenny didn't know what to do. She'd never kissed a man before. She had assumed he'd take over.

And then, suddenly, he groaned—or growled, she wasn't exactly sure which—low in his throat and did exactly what she wanted…and then some.

His arms came around her, crushing her body tightly against his hard muscular form. She caught her breath as feelings she'd never begun to imagine crashed through her, making her knees go weak and her stomach flutter alarmingly.

One hand moved up to her neck, cradling her head as his mouth took greater possession. Jenny clung to him, positive she could no longer stand on her own.

Dare coaxed her mouth open, drawing her very breath from her lungs. For a moment, she thought she would faint. Another moment passed and she thought she would expire if he didn't touch her.

The feelings she experienced were purely elemental, she told herself. They had nothing to do with the man that held her, kissed her. It had everything to do with the fact that Dare obviously knew what he was doing.

As the one hand cradled her head, the other moved up from her waist, traveling slowly, over her bodice. When his hand gently brushed the underside of her breast, Jenny stopped thinking. All she did was feel.

Dare gasped into her mouth when her small hands traveled somewhere they really shouldn't go. He tore his lips from hers, grabbed her hand, and stepped firmly away.

Dear God, it was the most difficult thing he'd ever done. She stood there in the pale moonlight, lips swollen from his kisses, eyes shining with promise and a little bit of wounded pride. More than anything, he wanted to take up where they'd left off, exploring every bare inch of her with his tongue.

A tremor wracked his body. If his thoughts continued in that particular vein, he'd do the unthinkable and take her right there on the ground, before the fountain—the ugliest, most unromantic fountain in existence.

"Jenny," he croaked. Clearing his throat, he tried again. "Jenny, I'm sorry, I don't know what came over me."

She snorted. He stared at her in utter disbelief. She

actually snorted. And it wasn't even one of those *ladylike* snorts.

"Please don't pretend it was your fault like a *proper gentleman*"—she said the words like a curse—"should. I was the one who initiated the embrace and as such, take the responsibility for it." She shrugged with apparent nonchalance.

He cocked his head slightly, studying her intently. "Very well, if that is what you wish. However, it was not your actions that made me take greater liberties than was offered."

"How stuffy you sound," she mused, smiling faintly. "I am astonished you failed to realize exactly what was being offered. Did you not receive my note?"

He moved a step closer, suddenly needing to see her eyes better. "I did. Why did you send it?"

"I would have thought that was plainly obvious."

His eyes widened. She couldn't possibly be suggesting…

Of course she could. She was Lady Genevieve Northwicke, insatiably curious, headstrong, willful Lady Genevieve Northwicke.

His temper flared. "Are you out of your mind? You asked for an assignation to…dear God, woman, you are insane!"

"No," she snapped right back. "I'm not insane. I'm lonely!"

That shut him up proper. He stared, unable to fathom the idea that the rich, cosseted blond beauty before him was lonely. People like her didn't get lonely. They surrounded themselves with other people just like them and talked about their money and possessions, never letting ordinary cares touch their sparkling existence.

"I thought…" she sighed deeply. "I just thought…you were, too."

"Oh, Jenny-love," he whispered, feeling her pain tear a hole in his chest, "that's no reason to indulge in something you should only share with your husband."

Their gazes met, held. Both were darkened by moonlight and bitter thoughts. Hers shimmered with repressed tears. He would not have been surprised if his did as well.

He wanted to take her in his arms, comfort her, but he knew if he touched so much as a strand of her honey-gold hair, his tenuous control would slip. He'd wanted her since he first met her and he suspected he always would. When a single tear slipped down her pale ivory cheek, he stepped forward, his control be damned.

Jenny, horrified at her confession, doubly horrified at her shattered pride, and triply horrified at her loss of control, fled.

The blasted ball continued on interminably. Dare finally grew weary of standing around, waiting for Jenny to reappear again. She'd left the ballroom several minutes ago, after what had appeared to be a heated argument with her brother and sister.

He hadn't liked the look on her face. In his experience, when someone's face took on that particular cast, said person was teetering on the brink of total breakdown.

And Jenny, sweet, charismatic, effervescent Jenny, was lonely.

He turned and walked in the direction she'd gone without really making the conscious decision to do so. He kept an eye out for her overprotective brother, not wanting to tangle with him, and another out for his own brother, knowing, without a doubt, that Miles would not *approve*.

After a few minutes of searching, Dare finally found Jenny, huddled up on a broad settee in what appeared to be an unused antechamber in the Riesley house. Everything was under Holland covers. Jenny had thrown back the one covering her perch.

Dare closed the door, locking it against unwelcome intruders, and approached her much the way one would a wounded deer.

He stood beside the sofa. "Jenny-love," he whispered. She looked up at him with such misery that he gasped. "Oh, Jenny. What could possibly be so bad to warrant such misery?"

A fresh torrent answered his question and she buried her face in her folded arms, shoulders shaking with the force of her sobs.

Dare could no longer keep his distance. Jenny was hurting and that was something he wouldn't stand for.

He eased down beside her, gently taking her in his arms. Smoothing his hands over her back, he asked, "Tell me what it is, Jenny-love. I'll make everything better."

She sniffled, lifted her head slightly and accepted the handkerchief he held out to her. After wiping her face— amazingly unmarked by her grief—she sniffled again.

"Con says I mustn't speak with you," she admitted after a long moment. "Gwen agrees. I have not seen any evidence that you are unworthy of my... friendship. But they wouldn't listen. Con mentioned a girl you seduced and left but I told him it was nonsense, that you would never do such a thing and—" she broke off at the expression on his face.

"What?" Her pale brows furrowed in confusion at his guilty silence. "Oh my. It's true? You seduced a gently bred girl and abandoned her? How could you?"

Dare stared at her, unable to allow her to place all the blame on him as everyone else had. He opened his mouth to offer what miserable little defense he had but she forestalled him.

Shaking her head, she decided, "No, it is as I told Con. Nonsense. If you…granted her your attentions, it was as much her fault as yours, I'm sure."

He stared at her, one black brow lifted in utter astonishment. "You would trust me…just like that? No explanation or defense on my part. Just your own belief that I would never seduce someone who was innocent."

Jenny offered a blinding smile. "Of course. You may be maddening at times, even less than gentlemanly at others, but you are not a scoundrel."

In that moment, Dare was quite sure he loved her. No one, not even his own twin, had ever taken his part in the whole miserable debacle. No one had trusted that there were circumstances that led to his behavior, not the least of which happened to be the fact that Belinda Markwell had honored half the county with her attentions and he had simply been yet another to fall for her dubious charms. It was moot that she had been only nineteen at the time.

"Thank you," he told Jenny now, from the bottom of his bitterly blackened heart.

It may not have actually been true before, but it was now.

Dare glared at his reflection. Seducer of innocents. Ruiner of reputations.

The devil incarnate.

After being told that he was honorable, what does he do? He seduces the one person who actually believed he wasn't like that.

He groaned. Memories of last night, Jenny, and pale moonlight spilling over silken skin coalesced in his mind, making him stumble blindly for a chair. How could he be so bloody stupid? He couldn't even blame drink, as he'd not had one all night.

Raking a hand through his sleep-mussed hair, he wondered bitterly if he had completely lost his mind. Lady

Genevieve Northwicke, beautiful, daughter-of-a-duke Jenny, was no longer an innocent virgin eagerly awaiting her husband's induction into the mysteries of the marriage bed. Oh no. She now knew exactly what would happen, with a few little extras thrown in for good measure.

He had taken his time with her, made her want him as he wanted her and when she had breathlessly begged him to take her, he'd readily complied, not even giving a thought to the fact that her family was only a few hundred feet away, dancing in the ballroom.

And it had been everything he could have dreamed. She was as passionate as he'd supposed, giving as well as taking, making him ache just to recall her words and actions. She'd excelled as a student, barely blushing at her inquisitive queries that bordered on indecent.

And he'd thrived in teaching her things he was sure she would probably never learn from whatever prosy old bore she ended up marrying.

She should be pledging her life to him, he thought with an inner snarl. But...

He really was the cad everyone thought him. And the worst part was, he couldn't marry her.

No matter how desperately he wanted to.

She deserved a man who could give her the world. A

man who wasn't tied down by obligations that took him away for months at a time. A man worthy of her and her station.

A man who wasn't considered the black sheep of a family that had its fair—*un*fair?—share of balmy members.

And if he wasn't there to distract her, she would have her chance at a better man.

He suppressed a growl at the thought of a *better* man touching her lily-white skin, having the right to see her naked, bring her pleasure, satisfy her every curious whim.

For the first time in his life, Dare wished the past undone. Worse than that, he wished he were Miles.

Rising, Dare dressed. His movements were precise, done without thought, mechanical. In less than an hour, he was packed.

Less than five minutes after that, he was gone.

Nine

The Prestwich household rose just after dawn as was their habit, to prepare the day's bread and begin the many other chores required to ensure the sufficient running of a house.

It was a day like any other. Except for the fact that when West scratched at Mr. Darius's chamber, he received no response.

It had become routine for the butler to serve Dare in whatever capacity he could. The young man's search for a valet had not gone well and while West openly disapproved of many of the young man's activities and attitudes, he also secretly liked Dare.

And so he stood outside the young master's door, a perplexed frown marring his normally rigid countenance. He entered the chamber, an action he would never have performed without permission had he not been so uneasy about the preternatural silence.

He was actually less than surprised when he saw the

tangled bedclothes, empty wardrobe…and two letters propped up on the washstand.

Bri sat up in bed, nibbling dry toast and trying very hard to keep her stomach firmly in place. She hadn't had morning sickness with any of her other pregnancies; why would she have it with this latest?

Annoyed, her command to enter was terse when there came a scratching at her door. West entered, holding two sheets of folded parchment in one hand.

"My lady, these were left by Mr. Darius."

Bri's eyebrows threatened to disappear into her curly red hair. Reaching out a hand, she demanded, "Where is he?"

"I'm sure I don't know, my lady."

Her ladyship scowled. "You know everything, West. How could Dare's precipitate flight get past you?"

"I'm sure I don't know."

Lady Prestwich shook her head at his evasive answer, opening the note labeled *Bri*. She quickly scanned the contents, swearing in such a way that even West, who had heard some rather colorful language from his unusual mistress, winced.

Without a thought to the impropriety of reading someone else's correspondence, Bri also read the other note. Instead of swearing, her face went unnaturally pale.

"Dear God, how could he?" she breathed.

She gasped suddenly, groping for the edge of the bed. West, a little out of his element in the lady's bedchamber, nevertheless realized she was trying to get to the chamberpot. He reached it before her and held it out as she emptied the nonexistent contents of her stomach.

In that moment, seeing his beloved mistress in such agony, West was quite sure he could have cheerfully strangled Mr. Darius Prestwich.

Lady Prestwich spent the rest of that day contemplating ways of murdering Dare that would cause him as much pain as humanly possibly.

She also wondered how the devil she was going to tell her husband while preventing him from doing much the same thing. She was quite sure she'd never be able to convince him.

Her thoughts went to Miles and she couldn't help but

wonder why Dare had not left a note for his twin. But then, they didn't behave as the few twins she knew; they seemed constantly at each other's throats and not in the brotherly fashion that most siblings were. Their rivalry seemed almost...bitter.

But mostly her thoughts centered on Lady Genevieve Northwicke. She knew the young lady well enough to know that her headstrong curiosity was probably as much or more to blame for her predicament than Dare was—not that she didn't place the bulk of the responsibility squarely upon the *gentleman's* shoulders.

Bri sighed, her shoulders slumping. Could she have been so very wrong about Dare? She had loved him from the first moment she met him, seeing in him a kindred spirit. He was injured inside, hurting, and using humor and wit—along with a healthy dose of biting sarcasm—to cover it up. He was everything she would have wanted in a brother and her sympathy for his feelings of self-doubt gave her an insight into his, sometimes, odd actions.

But now she wondered if perhaps she'd been very, very wrong about him. It irked her that she could so misjudge another person, especially one in the same family as her husband—the only other person she'd so grievously, and erroneously, reviled.

"Lady Connor Northwicke, my lady."

As thrilled as she always was to see her dearest friend, Bri nevertheless wished she had informed West that she was "not at home" to callers.

Rising, she embraced her friend warmly. "Verena! What brings you by? I wasn't even aware you were in Town yet."

Lady Verena, her violet eyes twinkling with some secret merriment, explained her sudden appearance. "Connor was lonely without me so he sent a retinue of servants to conduct me hither. I just arrived last night and so thought to come here immediately this morning." Her smile disappeared, replaced by concern. "Are you quite all right, my dear? You look peaked."

Bri glanced at the door. West lingered. "Tea, West." He bowed, withdrawing, silent as a ghost.

"Oh, Verena, I am in a quandary."

Moving to the settee, the two ladies sat, their arms linked companionably.

"Tell me, dear. What has you so troubled?"

Bri explained, her fingers uncharacteristically pleating and un-pleating the muslin of her skirts. When she realized what she was doing, she uttered an oath, apologizing immediately afterward.

"So, now I'm at an impasse. I can't tell Adam because nothing on earth will stop him from committing murder. And obviously, I can't tell Con as he would do much the same."

Verena's horrified look spoke volumes. "Are you sure? I mean...have you talked to Jenny?"

"Dare didn't come right out and confess anything in his note, but I assure you, the tone was far too intimate and apologetic to be otherwise."

"Oh dear," murmured Verena, her shoulders slumping just a bit. "This is quite a pickle, isn't it?"

Bri released a staccato laugh. "A pickle, yes. I'm just not sure what to do about it short of gelding Dare."

Verena was oddly silent, her dark brows creased in thought. "I'm not sure you need to *do* anything," she finally replied, slowly.

Bri leaned forward. "What do you mean?"

"Well, even if what you suspect it true, there may not be any consequences. Perhaps Jenny will emerge with little more than a loss of virtue."

"In other words, I hold my peace until we find out whether or not she's *enceinte*."

"Precisely."

"And the note?"

Verena's gaze was frankly puzzled. "What about it?"

Bri shrugged. "It's plain he doesn't want to marry her, or can't. I wonder if it would be wise to give her the note that he left. She may take it as a sign of his good regard despite the goodbye inherent in the message. Would it not be cruel to raise her hopes?"

"You feel she may move on if she believed his heart was not constant?" Bri nodded. Verena pondered that idea a moment. Then, "Would you have moved on had Adam done the same?"

"He's gone? Just like that? He said nothing?"

Realizing that her voice rose alarmingly with each word, Lady Genevieve took a deep calming breath. It would not do for her to lose her poise now.

She stared at Lady Brianna Prestwich hopefully, hardly daring to believe that Dare might have left something for her, some word, some sign that he was returning one day or that her feelings were reciprocated.

Bri shook her head, patting Jenny's hand. "No, dear, he said nothing. He was gone before the servants were even up this morning."

Jenny was sure her face was crumpling. She knew her heart was. It folded into itself until it resembled nothing more than a hard little stone.

After last night, he would just leave? Had he no honor after all? Dear God, she'd given him her virginity! The least he could do was stay and see how she fared.

A shiver traversed her spine at the memory of what he'd done to her. She wanted a repeat of the encounter even though she knew it was insane and wrong to want such a thing outside of marriage. It only led to heartache and illegitimate offspring.

"Are you cold, Lady Genevieve?" Bri asked solicitously.

Coming swiftly to herself, Jenny shook her head, denying the truth that she was indeed very cold—but from inside.

"Is anything wrong, Lady Genevieve?"

Jenny gave a jerky shake of her head, rising to her feet. She simply had to get away. If she stayed another moment, she would break down and cry.

He wasn't worth her tears, she told herself sternly. Accepting her outer clothing from the butler, she hurried out to her carriage.

She tried to shrug off the incipient pain, telling herself

she had to forget what happened between them and go on from there.

It became her mantra.

Lady Genevieve Northwicke was seen at all the *ton* events a person could possibly attend in one season. She could be found at four to five events in each evening, sparkling and shining as never before.

Society watched her in open curiosity, wondering at her odd behavior. She had always been a pleasant girl, but never had she so openly flirted and charmed her partners.

She seemed to show marked interest in Mr. Miles Prestwich, the significance of which was not lost on anyone. She had previously enjoyed an oddly close friendship with that gentleman's twin brother and it was universally acknowledged that she was nursing a broken heart.

Had Jenny been privy to any of these rumors, she'd have been horrified. As it was, she was so miserably lonely that she acted purely on instinct. Everything she said, everything she did was mechanical. She spent her days and evenings like an automaton, going through the motions of living without really experiencing any of it.

And yet, she would have been the first to deny a broken heart as her malady. Her pride would not let her admit that Dare had broken her heart, making her feel less than worthy.

A month after he left, with no word from him, Jenny finally gave up...at least, she told herself she did. He wasn't coming back, he'd moved on, forgotten her. She was nothing more than a convenient, there for his pleasure and cast aside.

How lowering.

Hyde Park was Society's showcase. It was there—in sparkling raiment and glittering jewels, with high-stepping cattle and flashy carriages—that the upper echelons preened like so many peacocks.

It was where Lady Genevieve Northwicke and her sister, Lady Guinevere shined. They usually rode with their brother and sister-in-law but occasionally they could be found in the company of whatever gentlemen had managed to catch their attention.

And they were inseparable as never before. Jenny

clung to her sister as if afraid to lose her. And Gwen, puzzled, clung right back, a niggling fear in the back of her mind telling her that something was very, very wrong.

Jenny laughed joyously, flirted modestly, and behaved properly at all times. But to anyone who cared enough to look beyond the surface, it was apparent in the cornflower blue of her eyes that she hid a deep and miserable fear.

It was her family who saw it, wondered at it, and privately attributed it to any number of female megrims. Lady Verena and Lady Prestwich, however, had a sinking feeling that they knew its cause and hoped against hope that they were mistaken.

It was while riding with Con and Verena that Jenny came to a startling realization. It had lingered in the back of her mind, festering for some weeks, but she'd managed to avoid giving the fear words.

And now, predictably while riding in such a public venue, it slammed into her full force, making her gasp for breath.

Lord Compton, her sometimes companion in the park, halted his dun mare, alarmed at the sudden pallor of his fair partner. Jenny also stopped, trying desperately to catch a breath but failing.

Lord Connor, alerted by Compton's shout, raced

forward, pulling to a stop beside his sister. She was gasping as if she were suffocating slowly. He threw himself from the saddle, grabbed her around the waist and hauled her down to sit on a nearby park bench. Pushing her head down ruthlessly between her knees, he ordered her tersely to calm down and breath, dammit!

Jenny tried. But the thoughts streaking through her brain quite simply would not allow her a single healing breath.

When she'd gone a full sixty seconds without a decent breath and her vision was turning black around the edges, her brother thumped her, none too gently, on the back.

Suddenly, her lungs began working properly again. She drew in one deep breath, then two, then three. Finally, Connor's anchoring hand was removed and she could sit up.

Staring in dismay, she realized she'd created quite a scene. Members of Society gathered all around trying none-too-subtly to determine what ailed her. Heads craned over and around other heads, mouths bent to whisper into neighbor's ears, and everyone formed some sort of conclusion. Mostly erroneous, but she just knew some of them were forming the right one.

And it almost terrified her into another fit.

"No, you don't, Jenny," snapped her brother. "Do not panic again." His voice rose a bit, in order to reach the front members of their unwelcome audience. "Bluebell merely stumbled. You were not about to be thrown."

Jenny thanked her brother for this unlikely excuse even as she cursed him for putting her equestrian skills in such a poor light. She'd always been a rather good rider but considering what the real problem was, she'd allow everyone to believe she had no business being on a horse.

Besides, wasn't it dangerous to ride in her condition? What if she *had* been thrown?

Jenny just barely refrained from clutching protectively at her stomach. Pasting a rather sickly smile on her pale features, she assured her brother in an undertone that all was well and she'd merely been overcome with faintness. His look was dubious but he accepted her excuse with good grace and helped her to stand.

They returned sedately to Denbigh House, Lord Compton bidding them adieu at the door. Lord Connor ushered his sisters into the house and into an empty receiving room with a terse order to sit.

Rounding on them, Jenny in particular, he asked, "What is going on?" He waved a hand in the air, his expression warning them to be honest. "And none of this feeling faint nonsense. You've never felt faint a day in your life."

Jenny looked indignant. "I have too. Remember Cousin Louisa's wedding?"

Connor grunted. "That hardly counts. I felt faint. Lord, who would have thought she'd have the nerve to wear a black dress to her own wedding."

Jenny and Gwen giggled helplessly. "Perhaps if she'd been marrying against her will but she honestly believed black was a becoming and appropriate color for a wedding," gasped Gwen.

"Do you know she said she didn't know what all the fuss was about," added Jenny. "She had no idea her bosom was about to fall out of her bodice."

The girls erupted into laughter and even Connor couldn't keep back a smile or two.

After a moment, his lordship finally inserted dimly, "That is not to the point and you know it. Then, holding back your laughter brought on your faintness. Today was utter panic." He paused, his gaze probing. With a sigh, he sat down on the settee between his sisters, making them edge closer to the arms. "Jenny, I have seen that look before and prayed to God then to never see it again. Please tell me what caused it."

Part of Jenny wanted desperately to do just that. Another part, the saner, more sensible part, knew that to tell her brother at this moment would be to sign Dare's death warrant.

"It was a momentary qualm, nothing more, dear brother," she said, kissing his cheek.

It was obvious from his expression that he would not be swayed, so she added, a little maliciously, "If you must know, it's my time and I felt a stomach cramp."

A snort came from Gwen, who knew that wasn't the case. Connor flushed a little, smiling self-deprecatingly. "I'm sorry I asked," he muttered.

He left a few moments later. Gwen turned to her sister. "He did not believe you, you know."

"I know," the elder of the twins sighed. "It was all I could think of that might make him stop questioning me."

Gwen stared at her mirror image for a long moment. "Will you tell me?"

Jenny stood and moved the to the long window overlooking the back gardens. She didn't really see anything beyond her own reflection in the leaded panes of glass.

Dropping her gaze to her clenched fingers, she whispered, "I'm pregnant."

Ten

When the silence lengthened to near-breaking point, Jenny turned. She regarded her sister in abject misery. She sniffed against incipient tears, determined to prevent their falling.

"Are you sure?" Gwen asked tonelessly. "Absolutely sure?"

Jenny nodded, a tear escaping to slide down her pale cheek. "I have missed my monthly twice. You know I've never missed one before."

"And you only just now realized?"

Jenny nodded.

"Dear God, what will we do? You can't have a... bastard. Father will kill us both."

"I don't know what to do."

Gwen threw her hands up in dismay. "I don't know what to tell you either! You will have to confess to Father." She bit her lip, distressed. "I just hope Con doesn't find out." Once again meeting her sister's eye, she asked, "Who is the father? No, wait, I know. It's Dare. How could he?"

Jenny's expression turned wry. "Can you blame him when I offered myself so freely? He is not to blame."

"Of course he is, you ninny! He is the gentleman; he should have shown some restraint."

Favoring her twin with a pitying look, Jenny retorted, "It is the lady's obligation to always maintain distance and modesty with an unmarried gentleman. Who do you believe Society will blame, Gwen? Father and Con may place the responsibility squarely on Dare's shoulders, but they still treat us as though we have just emerged from the schoolroom."

"And you have just proven they have reason to do so," Gwen snapped. Turning on her heel, she left the room, closing the chamber door with an angry click.

Jenny sank down on settee, her eyes again filling with miserable tears. She wanted Dare to magically appear and make everything all right.

But that wasn't going to happen. He was gone only God knew where doing only God knew what.

And Jenny was left here, carrying a precious burden inside her that she wanted more than she'd ever wanted anything in her life. Except...

Except, she wanted Dare there to share it with her.

It was with something of a passive sensation that Jenny realized the Empire waist style so popular was to her benefit. Although her stomach was still the same as ever, she knew it would not be long before her pregnancy would begin to show.

If only she could keep her secret until the last possible moment.

Alas for 'if onlys'. It was two days after she confessed to her sister that her mother approached her, a militant gleam in her blue eyes.

Jenny halted on her way to the library, her stance nearly as defiant as her expression.

"Mother?" she inquired in as polite a tone as she could muster.

"Genevieve, may I have a word with you?"

Jenny dutifully followed her mother to the latter's sitting room. Lady Denbigh's choice of setting merely concreted Jenny's supposition that her mother knew.

Her surety was further supplemented when her mother sat but offered no chair to her daughter.

"Is there something you'd care to tell me, Genevieve?"

"What could I tell you that you don't already know?" the girl asked flippantly.

"I will thank you to watch your tone with me, young lady," her mother snapped back. "I heard an ugly rumor but, knowing you as I do, I discounted it as mere maliciousness. Your attitude leads me to believe otherwise."

Jenny sighed. "Pray accept my sincere apologies, Mama. What have you heard?"

The duchess's face softened. "Sit down, dear." She waited a moment until her daughter complied. "It has come to my attention that you have behaved... improperly... with a certain gentleman of our acquaintance."

Jenny's lips twisted in something akin to actual humor. It was almost amusing to hear her mother describe her fall from grace in such a roundabout way.

"Mother, if you are asking whether I tossed my virtue away on a man hardly worth my time, let alone my affections, it is, unfortunately, true."

It almost pained her to see the misery attach itself to her mother's lovely countenance. But she was too far steeped in her own despair and fears to pay much heed to what she caused others.

The duchess sighed hugely. "It is true?" Her voice was

so faint, Jenny had to strain to hear. "Is that the end of it? Is there more?"

A bit of Jenny's flippant attitude returned. "What more could there possibly be, Mother? I gave him my virginity and he left the next day. Well, that very day, if you'd care to be precise about it. So he cannot be forced to marry me since no one knows where he is."

"Not even his brother?"

Jenny studied her mother's fine-boned features. "No, Miles does not know where he is. Gwen would have told me else."

Lady Denbigh's eyes filled with tears of frustration and pain. "And if he knew about the child? Would he come then?"

"No. I'm sure he would run farther away."

"There is nothing to be done then. You will have to go to another country to have the child, leave it there and return to a semblance of your former life."

"No."

The duchess was speechless. Her wide blue eyes grew until they dominated her face. "Excuse me?"

Jenny remained adamant although her surprise at her own declaration threatened to undo her. "I said no. No, I will not go away. No, I will not give up my baby. No, I will not return as if nothing happened. No."

"But, darling, you have to. How else will you survive the ostracism?"

The younger woman's face grew pensive. "You are right," she relented. Her mother's features relaxed until Jenny added, "I will have to leave Town at least. Society may say what they wish about me but I don't need to be around to hear it. I will not give up my child."

That evening before dinner, Jenny was told to wait upon her father's pleasure in his study. She had some misgivings but was determined to hold to her decision to keep her baby.

The duke was seated behind his desk, perusing some paper that had him frowning mightily. Jenny hesitated, not wanting to interrupt, but he must have heard her enter.

"Sit down, child."

Inside, she relaxed just a bit. If he'd been truly upset, he'd not have called her that.

She sat, arranging her skirts just so. When she looked up, her father was watching her, the look of disappointment in his gray eyes like a slap in the face.

Her breath caught on a sob. "I'm sorry, Papa. I truly am."

His look didn't change. "I'm sure you are. Now. Hindsight ever was perfect."

An uncomfortable silence fell in which Jenny wanted to make excuses… but she had none to give. She'd made a mistake and now she'd have to pay the price of her actions.

Finally, after what seemed like hours but was in fact only minutes, the duke said, almost conversationally, "Your mother tells me you will not give up the child."

"No, sir, I will not."

He seemed a little surprised at her firm tone. "You do realize, of course, that this will affect our whole family."

"Yes, sir, I do."

"And this may affect Gwen's chances at a good match."

Jenny swallowed painfully. "I understand."

"And yet, you would bring scandal down on all our heads just so you can have your live doll to play with when you feel like it and put away when you're bored with it."

Jenny shot to her feet. "NO! I want this child because it's mine. Because it has more opportunity for happiness with me than some poor family who already has a dozen mouths to feed. Because it's a part of Dare and is the only part I'll ever have." Her words ended on a strangled sob. She pressed her fingers to her lips, willing the choking tears back.

"Selfish reasons, to be sure," her sire said callously.

Jenny merely nodded, admitting at least that much.

"And yet, I wonder," the duke mused. "If you gave the child up, you could go on as if nothing occurred. You could pretend you had not borne a child out of wedlock, go to parties, and make a brilliant match. In short, you could forget your mistake and most likely learn nothing from it… a far more selfish decision, if one were to think about it."

A moment of taut silence followed. The duke watched his daughter intently but dispassionately. Jenny stared down at her hands, trying to form the words she needed to say and make her father understand.

"I would have the responsibility of my indiscretion, my lord," she whispered. "I need the responsibility of my indiscretion. I need this baby and this baby needs me."

"Will you love the child, my girl? Or will you berate it every day of its life for being born?"

Looking him directly in the eye, she vowed, "I will love this child with every beat of my heart and every breath in my body." She paused to swallow another rising sob. Her next words were barely heard over the sudden commotion in the hall outside the study. "I already do."

Lord Connor Northwicke was fit to be tied. He'd heard through an acquaintance that Jenny had managed to get herself in serious trouble. Threatening to call the man out for slandering his sister had only resulted in pitying glances that had further enraged him.

Now, Connor wanted the truth. He stomped into his father's townhouse, shaking rainwater from his hair having conveniently forgotten his hat. The icy rivulets running beneath his collar did not help his mood.

The duke's butler was properly impassive, taking the young lord's coat and gloves and informing him that his grace, the duke was in conference with Lady Genevieve in the study.

"I'll announce myself," he told the butler coldly. He moved to the study in the back of the ground floor. The staccato beat of his footsteps accurately portrayed the dangerous depths to which his mood had sunk.

He paused outside the door, took a deep breath to try to calm himself, and knocked once. He opened the door even as his father was bidding him to do so.

"I apologize, Father, for bursting in on you like this."

His glance found his sister's weeping form and he cursed. He didn't bother to apologize even with the duke's admonishing eye silently reprimanding him.

"I'll kill the blighter!"

Jenny surged to her feet, her own temper ignited. "You will not, Connor! You will leave him to live whatever life he chooses. If he doesn't want me, that's his choice."

He ignored her, addressing their father. "You can't possibly let him get away with this, sir."

The duke merely lifted an eyebrow as he slowly stood. "What can I do, short of hunting Prestwich down? Adam has not been around so I'm sure does not know his whereabouts nor does Miles."

"Then I'll do it."

"Where do you propose to start looking, Con?" Denbigh asked reasonably. Then, surprisingly, he added, "I've had runners looking for the young man. Darius does not want to be found. It's as if he never existed."

For some reason, instead of increasing his temper, as such tidings should, Connor's anger swiftly deflated. He slumped into a seat next to Jenny's, heedless of the rudeness of sitting while a lady was standing.

"It simply cannot be left this way," he muttered. "She

cannot go through the hell in store for her. She must have a husband."

Jenny sat, her depression once again settling upon her like a shroud. "I will survive, Con. You needn't take on my woes as your own."

He turned his head to look at her. She flinched at the angry disappointment still visible in his blue eyes. "Needn't I? It is up to me to defend your honor, as your brother and Father's heir. What does it say about me that I do not do so?"

"I admit I was wrong. But I am as much at fault as Dare. And if he sees fit to stay away, there is nothing anyone can do about it."

"Where will you go to have the child?"

"Home," she answered decisively. "I will go back to Denbigh Castle." Her eyes met those of her father. "And if I am not welcome there, I shall make my way somewhere else. I have my legacy from Grandmother and it is sufficient to keep a small house."

Her father nodded and she was relieved. He had the right to deny her the inheritance since she had yet to reach the age of five-and-twenty.

He added, "You may return to Denbigh, however, if you choose."

Connor regarded his father with astonishment. "You can't be serious, Father! She will be ostracized until she flees or takes her own life."

"She is aware of that, Con. She has decided the child will stay with her and she will be its mother. We cannot convince her otherwise." He sounded oddly proud of that fact.

Connor simply sat there and gaped, his mouth opening and closing a few times before he finally managed to sputter, "But her life will be ruined. She doesn't deserve that."

Jenny, having had about all she could take of being ignored, snapped, "I am aware of that, and I'll thank you to at least pretend I am here. As to my deserving it or not, that is beside the point. Would you have me simply discard my responsibility because I am female? Not only female but the daughter of a powerful peer, and in so being, that option is open to me? A female who was naïve enough to be... seduced... by pretty words and whispered promises? Which, by the bye, is far from the truth."

Both gentlemen stared at her. "You were forced?" they asked in unison.

"No, I wasn't forced. I seduced him," she asserted firmly. "I have told you over and over that I am as much to blame, more so even than Dare, but you insisted on placing the lion's share of the responsibility squarely on his shoulders."

The duke's softly spoken reply overrode whatever she may have added. "That is the way of the social sphere to which we belong. To go against their rules is to court utter ruin."

She sighed, staring down at her clasped hands. "I know. And I'm willing to do that. My only regret is the shame I bring to my family."

The duke and his son shared a long look.

"By the way, Con," Jenny asked, her brow furrowed in thought, "how did you hear about this? Did Father tell you, or Mother, perhaps?"

"Neither, actually. I'd like to think Father would have seen fit to inform me eventually but, unfortunately, it was Lord Compton who told me the latest rumors flying about."

She released a weary breath. "So, it begins." She stood, forcing her male relatives to stand as well. "I shall go and have Alice pack for my departure. I shall inform you presently where I've decided to reside."

She left the room, her spine straight, her face expressionless. The door closed with a silent click behind her.

Eleven

When a tearful Lady Guinevere informed Miles that her sister was in trouble and it was his brother's fault, his heart plummeted.

It was Belinda Markwell all over again— only much, much worse.

He had hoped Dare had learned from that experience and gained wisdom in his dealings with the fair sex. Apparently, he hadn't.

After receiving reassurance that Lady Genevieve would never resort to suicide, Miles relaxed somewhat. He was even slightly amused by Gwen's vehemence on the subject.

And now, with Gwen having returned to her home, Miles had time to contemplate exactly what such scandal would mean for their families. He was positive the duke's family would survive; such was the way of the titled elite.

It was Adam who would suffer the brunt. This latest gossip added to what still surrounded Bri would make their acceptance in Society exactly nil.

He scoffed at his own musings. It wasn't as if Adam or Bri would care. They'd courted scandal for years.

Still, Miles had his mother and father to think about as well. While they were not in the habit of even visiting London, much less attending *ton* events, he was quite sure they wouldn't appreciate having the choice taken from them. Who would?

The real fear was what it would do to the relations between Adam's and the duke's families. Denbigh had practically raised Adam, who had spent holidays there when he and Connor were down from school. It was Denbigh who'd bought a commission for Adam in Wellington's army and Denbigh who'd been proud of all the baronet had accomplished. Denbigh was like a father to Adam.

But this, Adam's cousin having taken the innocence of one of Denbigh's daughters, just might make their past relationship precarious. And Miles knew Lord Connor would hold Adam somewhat responsible for what Dare had done. How could he not?

But what could be done? The girl needed a husband and quickly. Dare was not available to be prevailed upon—and despite all that had occurred, Miles was quite sure his

Redemption

brother would not hesitate to rescue her.

Jenny was nothing like Belinda, after all, Miles reflected wryly. His fingers idly caressed the inkwell on his desk. Miles had not known at the time that Belinda had had a penchant for loose behavior but he'd learned not long after her body was discovered, poisoned. It had been ruled a suicide but Miles had his suspicions. The girl had been pregnant, something that was not conducive to her particular activities. Miles was sure she had tried to abort the baby and had miscalculated the strength of the drug she'd taken.

But none of that was too the point. Jenny would never do such a thing and Gwen assured him she was determined to raise her child herself. Which left only one option.

Acting decisively, as was his wont, Miles Prestwich rose and shrugged into his coat. Five minutes later, he was on his way to visit the Duke of Denbigh.

The duke actually agreed to speak with Miles, an unlooked-for compliment to the young man, under the circumstances.

Miles was not surprised by Lord Denbigh's stony

expression nor was he altogether taken unaware when he was told curtly to state his reason for being there.

Miles refrained from asking for a seat. He was there to make amends, not beg forgiveness on behalf of his brother.

"I have been made aware of Lady Genevieve's situation, your grace," he said without any roundaboutation.

The duke's raised eyebrow was his only answer.

With an inward sigh, he continued, "If it is agreeable to you, your grace, I'd like to try to make amends."

"And how, young man, could you possibly do that?"

"I will marry her, give her child a name and, hopefully, avert the worst of the scandal."

His grace's face underwent a series of emotions so quickly that Miles couldn't name one before it was promptly replaced with another.

The duke finally settled on incredulity. "You would do that? Why?"

"My family's honor is at stake here, too, your grace," he said simply.

A sneer twisted Lord Denbigh's lips. "Snagging a duke's daughter, even a ruined one, would be quite a coup for you."

Miles maintained an icy dignity although he was tempted to sneer right back. "Would you rather have a fortune-hunter or a Cit as a son-in-law? I, at least, offer a genteel background and enough income to live in comfort."

"My daughter says she will not marry."

Miles frowned. "She would choose to live the life of a fallen woman, ruined with a bastard child, instead of marrying a worthy gentleman who only wants to help salvage some of the damage wrought?"

"You will have to ask her that yourself." Denbigh studied the young man for several long moments before adding dismissively, "You will find Jenny in the morning room."

The announcement in the morning papers rocked London. Everyone was agog over the news that the hitherto ruined Lady Genevieve Northwicke had gone and trapped herself a husband.

It was mentioned in more than one home, over steaming morning chocolate and toast, that dukes ever were a law unto themselves. It was only natural that Daddy Denbigh would buy his despoiled child a way out of her shame.

Slightly more intriguing was the choice of bridegroom.

None other than the twin brother of the very man whispered to have ruined the girl. Many a footman overheard the remark that it was only fitting, under the circumstances.

Jenny read the announcement with a sense of doom. How could she have actually agreed to marry the brother of the man she loved? The very man she strongly suspected held her own twin sister's heart?

Suddenly clamping a hand to her mouth, Jenny slid to the edge of her bed in search of the chamber pot. It was normal for her to feel queasy in the morning but never had she actually emptied her already painfully empty stomach.

She rinsed her mouth and leaned back, wiping her lips with her handkerchief.

It was a stupid plan, she admitted ruefully. She had only agreed to marry Miles because she hoped that Dare would see the notice and come haring back to claim her himself. It was selfish and immature to use him so and Gwen was being hurt in the process.

Oh, would she never learn?

It worked.

Unfortunately, not quite the way she had planned.

Dare did, indeed, come haring home just as soon as he received word of his brother's impending nuptials...to none other than the woman he, not Miles, loved.

Dare couldn't stop himself from hying back to London, determined to find answers.

Questions plagued him as he urged his hired nag to greater speeds. Had Jenny's family discovered their little... indiscretion? Had she told them, or perhaps her sister had? It never even occurred to him that she might not have told her twin. Had Miles felt obligated, as his brother, to right the wrong he'd done the lady?

And not once in his disturbed imaginings, did he ever consider that she was pregnant.

West opened the door at the knock and almost closed it again when he realized who it was.

Dare would have laughed had he not been so shocked to see the look of outrage on the imperturbably butler's august countenance. As it was, he barely had enough time to stick his foot in the door.

"West, I came as soon as I could. Please let me pass."

West held his ground for a second before saying

peevishly, "I shouldn't let you by, Master Dare, knowing what you did. I should have the footmen throw you in the Serpentine."

"Yes, you should, West," Dare agreed wholeheartedly. Then he waited.

West sighed and opened the door. "I would welcome you, Master Dare, but I'm afraid you are not."

"Understandable, my good man. Now, do you take these"—holding out his riding crop, coat, hat, and gloves—"or do I make do for myself?"

"I should refuse to assist you," the butler grumbled, "but I find myself unable to do so." He took Dare's things from him and disappeared into the furthest recesses of the house.

Dare waited. He knew his twin, and he knew Miles would know he was there. He would be down to... probably hit him, momentarily.

Dare glanced around the open foyer and sat in a chair against the wall. He wondered where the footman had got to who was supposed to be sitting there. Probably off informing the house that the "prodigal" returned, he though wryly.

Leaning back, he closed his eyes briefly, knowing what a precarious position such an action would put him in. His mind whirled back and forth over the events of the past months. Part of him, now, had no idea why he'd ever run in the first place. He should have stayed and at least tried to convince Jenny's family that he was worthy of being her husband.

His lips twisted cynically. He should not have touched her that night, invitation or not.

He heard a step a moment later. His eyes opened slowly to see his brother bearing down on him, fury emanating from his every pore. If Dare hadn't been the target of that anger, he'd have laughed.

Standing, he said, "And how is the happy bridegroom? Have you married her yet?"

He dodged the fist aimed at his face, but only just. The next fist met with his hand. He clenched his fingers over it, in far better physical shape than his bookworm brother was.

"Let go," snapped Miles.

Dare released him with a little jerk, nearly toppling the other man to the ground.

"I will allow that you have every right to hit me, Miles. But I will not let you do so here."

Miles nearly growled. Dare was amazed at how different he was behaving. His brother, the epitome of gentlemanly conduct, was acting like an animal.

He couldn't help it. He laughed. And Miles lunged for him.

Backing quickly away, Dare said placatingly, "Miles, I assure you, you can beat me as much as you want. Later. Right now, I need to know why you've promised to marry Jenny."

Miles took a deep breath, trying to calm his rage. "Yes, oddly enough, you are right. We should not do this here." He sent a significant look toward the back of the domicile where, Dare was quite sure, a group of very interested servants hovered.

Moments later, the two brothers were standing in Adam's study. Dare glanced around, asking, "Has Adam returned yet?"

"No. Bri said Lord Derringer was found and Adam remained there for a while to patch a few things up." He turned, facing his brother with the stoicism for which he was well known. "And where have you been?"

"America, mostly," he shrugged. "I was in Bath, on my way back, when I picked up a London paper over a week old. Imagine my surprise," he finished dryly.

"Damn your surprise, man! I'm engaged to Jenny because you were not here to fix your mess. Tell me, Dare. Will it always be up to me to clean up after you?"

"I don't understand what the big tragedy is, Miles."

Miles's eyes widened until they threatened to pop. Dare's grew, too, reflexively.

Then, abruptly, Miles frowned. "You don't know. No, how could you?" he muttered to himself.

It was Dare's turn to frown. And he did. With great displeasure. "What don't I know?"

"Sit down, Dare."

Dare wasn't sure he wanted to comply but decided the news would be bad no matter what he did. So he sat.

Miles didn't. He started pacing. Yet another action so unlike his brother that Dare grew very worried indeed.

Trying to lighten the mood, he quipped, "Miles, this behavior is very unbecoming in a gentleman. You make me dizzy to watch you."

Miles stopped abruptly, glaring. His next words were cruelly blunt, angered as he was by his twin's continued disregard for what was a very serious matter.

"Jenny's pregnant."

Twelve

Dare stared at his brother, uncomprehending. He blinked twice, slowly. Then, "Excuse me?"

"You heard me," snapped Miles. He sat in the chair behind the desk, glowering at Dare all the while. He refused to say more.

Dare was having trouble breathing. His neckerchief felt too tight and he was quite sure his face was turning purple. His mind just couldn't wrap itself around the idea that Jenny, his Jenny, was going to have a baby.

"Is it mine?" he asked, stupidly.

A very foul word passed his brother's lips. "I should kill you outright for that, Dare," he said through gritted teeth.

Dare shook his head, muttering, "No, of course it is. She would never…"

"No, she wouldn't."

Seeming to find some sort of relief in this firm statement, Dare nodded. "No, she wouldn't. I know she wouldn't."

"Dare, I can't break the engagement," Miles said, almost gently.

Dare started. "Why the hell not?" He almost came out of his chair in his agitation.

Dare had not actually thought about Miles breaking the engagement. But now that the subject was out for an airing, he wanted to know why. Jenny was his, after all, not Miles's.

Miles sighed as if the weight of the world rested on his shoulders. "She was ruined before, based solely on rumor, but if I jilt her now, she will be ruined solely on fact. Not to mention Gwen will die an old maid. Even now, her chances of marriage are not good."

Dare cursed himself. Miles was in love with Gwen. It was in the way he said her name with a bittersweet hopelessness. Dare had always suspected as much but his brother's inflection merely assured him that it was fact.

"Miles, break the engagement. I'll marry her. You can marry Gwen."

Miles shot his brother a disgusted look. "Do you honestly believe Denbigh would let me marry Gwen? She's the one who *didn't* disgrace herself. She may still have a chance at a good alliance. Jenny, on the other hand, has no chance and the duke will accept me as a son-in-law to satisfy family honor."

"Honor ever was overrated," grumbled Dare.

"The very fact that you feel that way proves you have none. Of course, impregnating Jenny proved that very well anyway."

Dare gave his brother a steady look. "I've often wondered if you've actually wanted me to beat you to a bloody pulp. Now more than ever."

"Beating me will not make me break the engagement," Miles sneered.

"I would do it purely for pleasure, I assure you." Rising, Dare prowled around, looking for anything with enough alcohol to numb at least some of his rioting emotions. Predictably, Adam's office was bare of liquid refreshment since Miles was the only one who really used the room.

"Dammit, why can't you have even one blasted bottle of something in here? I'd swear you were a monk except even they would drink wine."

A scratching at the door interrupted Miles's retort. West entered with a tray, a bottle, and one glass. He bowed before Dare, a slight smile tugging at his lips.

Dare quirked an eyebrow at the old man. "Listening at

doors again, West, my good man? No matter. I'll forgive you much for bringing me this." His grin left little doubt as to his sincerity.

The butler actually smiled fleetingly. "I wasn't listening, Master Dare. I anticipated. As is my obligation." He snapped a short bow and left the two gentlemen alone.

"I notice he brought only the one glass. Are you a monk, then?"

Dare glanced at Miles and was surprised at the sardonic smile twisting his brother's lips. "I assure you, brother, I am not. West knows I do not drink."

Dare poured and quaffed two fingers of some of the best Irish whisky he'd ever had. It crawled into his belly, unfurling a pleasing warmth that soon spread to his extremities. The comfort was immediate and nearly complete. For complete comfort, he'd need to find a way out of the mess he'd created. He poured another drink instead.

"You do not drink," Dare mused, swirling the liquid in the glass. He stared reflectively into the amber depths. "You do not smoke. You do not gamble. You do not indulge your passions. You do not use foul language." He paused, eyes raised just above the glass but not actually fixed on anything. Then, they swiveled just a bit to meet his twin's.

"No, I am mistaken. You do use foul language. Very foul indeed." His eyes were silently laughing.

"You're a bloody bastard, Dare."

At that, Dare laughed. "No, brother," he said, facetiously taking Mile's statement literally, "I am as legitimate as you are, I assure you."

Miles didn't deign to reply.

Dare released a bitter laugh. "I suppose this is the price we all pay for my sins. Astounding that I could have so much effect on the world at large, is it not?"

Again, Miles said nothing.

Dare uttered an oath that made Miles's earlier one seem tame in comparison. His fingers tightened alarmingly around his glass, the knuckles turning white. He was tempted to dash the thing against the hearth, but refrained. Barely. He carefully set the receptacle on the desk.

In a movement as agitated as his thoughts, he pushed his hand through his hair ripping the riband out to drop forlornly to the carpet. "Why do you calmly accept things the way they are?" he raged. He fisted his hands on his hips, dark hair wildly askew. "You don't want to marry her any more than, I'll warrant, she wants you. And anyone with half a brain can see you want Gwen. Why the devil do you sit there on your hands?"

Miles stood up halfway through this tirade. His hands were braced on the desk as if he would leap it and go for Dare's throat.

Somehow managing to maintain calm despite his fury, Miles explained in a clipped voice, "Do you not think one wastrel in the family is quite enough? If I do not obey Society's strictures, our entire family will be shamed."

"Who bloody well cares for Society, anyway!"

"I do!" Miles paused, swallowing. "Jenny and Gwen do as well."

Dare sighed. "Miles, you don't really care and you know it. Jenny and Gwen find the Season tedious and dull and you know that, too. How can you throw away your happiness for my miserable mistake?"

Miles slumped back into his chair. "It's just not that simple, Dare."

"Tell me."

A sigh of deep weariness escaped Miles's throat. "Do you know what it's like," he began softly, staring into his brother's eyes, "to be related to you?"

"A constant trial, I've little doubt."

Miles lips tipped up slightly at the corners. "True," he murmured. "A constant trial. Always doing whatever you want; never stopping to consider the consequences; forever landing yourself in more trouble with each passing day than the one previous. And everyone looking to me to fix it. Always. And still, at eight-and-twenty years old, you manage to land yourself in the biggest pickle yet: you seduced and impregnated a duke's daughter. For the sanity and well-being of all those involved, I beg you to not interfere."

"I can't just pretend like nothing happened. I can't just pretend I never... knew her." He hated the tone of defeat in his voice but was powerless to eliminate it. "Break the betrothal, Miles."

Miles shook his head almost regretfully. "I cannot, Dare. It's just not done. Do not try to convince me otherwise."

Dare studied his twin closely. He was confused and irritated by all he'd just been told. Then there was the fact that Jenny was having his child and instead of being the father, he would only be an uncle. The mere thought was galling.

Dare escaped to his room for a precious few minutes of blessed peace. He wondered where Bri's sharp tongue was and thanked God for its absence. She was either so livid she couldn't control her murderous impulses or she was actually gone from home.

Throwing clothes in every conceivable direction as he went, Dare walked into the water closet off his room and turned the water on to fill the tub. He thanked God for such a convenience and Adam for being freethinking enough to have it installed despite Society's odd feelings on bathing. Sinking down into the steaming water, he laid his head back and closed his eyes. He felt grimy and... old.

A bone-weary sigh pushed up his windpipe to escape in what a less compassionate person might call a sob. He managed to stifle the next one despite the overwhelming urge he had to break down and snivel like an infant.

It was several minutes later that Dare again opened his eyes. He realized a trifle ruefully that he must have fallen asleep. He wasn't surprised. He'd rode like the hounds of hell had dogged his heels. It was a wonder he'd made it without suffering a severe case of madness.

He laughed painfully. Perhaps that was what ailed him now. No, he was honest enough to admit the fair Jenny was what ailed him now. He wanted her as he'd never wanted another woman. The one time he'd been with her had haunted him ever since. And now...

Now, she was having his baby. He felt a slow smile stretch across his lips. In spite of everything, he was pleased. Being with her always and being allowed to acknowledge the child as his would make his life finally worth living.

Hell, if he had all that, his life would be bloody well perfect.

Adam returned to London that very evening. He found his house in a bit of an uproar, his wife upbraiding Dare while Miles stood by, watching grimly. Three servants stood a little way off, their eyes round as saucers.

Adam gave them one meaningful look, and they swiftly departed. With the departure of the menials came an embarrassed but defiant silence on Bri's part, a brooding one on Dare's, and a look of absolute relief on Miles's.

"Anyone care to explain?" he asked mildly, a sure sign he was well on his way to being *upset.*

Bri threw her hands up. "I give up. You deal with him." And she stormed out, slamming the door behind her.

"I apologize, Adam," Dare said quietly. "I never meant to upset her. Especially in her condition."

Miles glared at his twin. "You should have thought of that before," he said evenly, back in firm control of his emotions. He, too, took his leave, managing to close the door behind him with a snap rather than an all-out slam.

Adam gave Dare a long look. "Care to explain that cryptic statement?" he asked, his voice having gained the silkiness that suggested he was most *displeased.*

Dare just stared at him for a long moment. His face held not a hint of the emotions churning within him. He was the lowest despicable cad—and he knew it. He didn't need his cousin telling him what he already knew.

Even knowing the reaction his confession would cause, Dare nevertheless stated, calmly and clearly, "Miles is engaged to marry Lady Genevieve Northwicke… because she is pregnant… with my child… and I could not be found to do right by her."

Adam's eyes narrowed to dangerous little slits. "You… did…WHAT!?" Each word was separated, drawn out, the last one ending on an explosion of sound that threatened to rock the house on its foundation.

Dare neither said nor did a thing. He just waited. He knew what was coming, physically and mentally bracing himself.

Two seconds later, Adam's fist connected with his jaw. Dare barely moved. He favored his cousin with a blank stare, calmly pulling his handkerchief from his pocket. He pressed it to his bleeding lip.

"Have you nothing to say?" the baronet finally snapped.

"I have no defense, Adam," was Dare's softly spoken reply.

He wanted to hit him again. Dare could see the desire on Adam's face and was mildly surprised when his cousin restrained himself.

"What did Con say?" The older man's tone was back to calm, and infinitely dangerous.

"He threatened to hunt me down, of course, but refrained since Miles so gallantly offered for her."

His tone was utterly devoid of emotion. He was shocked he could keep the pain from his words. His brother was going to marry Lady Genevieve Northwicke. The only woman who'd ever made him feel even remotely worthy of life. The only woman, who, after hearing his pathetic story, offered friendship and redemption for his battered heart.

The only woman he'd ever love.

And he, damned idiot that he was, ran away, scared out of his mind by the emotions she made him feel.

"She must surely hate me," he said softly, hardly aware he'd spoken aloud.

Adam's head snapped up. The defeated tone in his young cousin's voice gave him pause. Was it possible…

Did the clunch actually love the girl?

Taking care to modulate his tone, he asked, "Why did you run?"

Dare released a short, infinitely bitter laugh, shoving his hand through his hair. "How could I stay? She would have expected marriage and I have nothing to give her."

"You have amassed enough wealth to get by," Adam pointed out dryly.

"Yes, wealth," Dare murmured. "I also bring with me a past so black, no father would dare give his daughter into my keeping. And she is the daughter of a duke."

"Perhaps. But you never know until you ask," he told him philosophically. "Nothing ventured, nothing gained... and all that rot."

"'Faint heart never won fair lady.'" Dare treated his cousin to a look of incredulous amazement. "Do you know what he said when Miles offered? He told him he wasn't what he wanted for his daughter. Miles, the perfect, never-done-wrong son and brother, every woman's dream husband, every father-in-law's dream son. What do you think Denbigh would say should I approach him and say, 'Please, sir, may I have your daughter to wife?' He wouldn't even deign to reply to such an outrageous request. He'd take one look at me and release the hounds."

"That's not necessarily true," Adam remarked casually. He moved to a chair and sat, leaning on the arm with a thoughtful expression on his face. "Denbigh would have been willing to accept you as Jenny's husband. Con may have had a few objections but Denbigh is wiser than most fathers of the elite class."

Dare stared blankly at Adam. "Meaning?"

"Meaning, you bloody nodcock, Denbigh would have realized you're in love with the girl and given you his blessing." One corner of his lips tipped up in a mocking smile. "After threatening to draw and quarter you for any future pain you may cause her."

The younger man suddenly sat, unheeding of where he stood in the room. Thankfully, there was a sofa right behind him. He couldn't say anything around the lump in his throat and had nothing to say to Adam's half-hearted jest since he barely heard it anyway.

Adam sighed softly. "But it's too late now, isn't it?"

Dare nodded once, a jerky movement that threatened to jilt his head from his shoulders. A headache blossomed behind his eyes and at the base of his neck.

Forcing his voice to work, he admitted, "I tried to convince Miles to break the betrothal. He refused."

Raising one eyebrow, Adam asked, "Does he care so

much for her then?"

"Not so much as the fact that he is Miles and will do no wrong if he can avoid it."

Adam snorted out a laugh. "Right, of course. Miles can't jilt a girl he's engaged to marry. It would go against everything he's ever believed in or held dear. Bloody boring if you ask me."

"Yes, well, I won't give up. If he marries Jenny, what about Gwen? I won't marry her, settling for the mirror image of the woman I really want. And she wants Miles. She has since she first met him."

Adam regarded his young cousin thoughtfully. "It is a problem, is it not?"

Thirteen

His trial by fire was far from over. Bri got her claws into him moments after he'd closed the door to his chamber. She forced her way in, her hands on her hips and green eyes blazing. The door was slammed firmly in her wake.

Smiling faintly, he observed, "It's hardly proper for you to be in my bedchamber alone with me, Bri. What will the servants think?"

"Fine time to be worrying about that," she snapped, clearly beside herself with rage. She closed her eyes and took a few deep breaths, trying to control her anger. After a concentrated effort, during which Dare remained wisely silent, she opened her eyes, pinioning him with a look.

"Tell me, Dare, was it worth it?"

Startled by her question, he asked, "What?"

What she uttered was a series of vulgar words that even Dare hesitated to use. His face flushed against his will even as he grinned at her.

"Do you kiss Adam with that mouth?"

He was quite sure his ears blistered after she favored him with a reply. He raised his hands in surrender. "You win, Bri. Dear God, you must have been a sailor in your checkered past."

His comment made her smile. "I could have been, make no mistake."

She paced over to the one chair in the chamber, seating herself with regal dignity. She took a moment to smooth the pale yellow-green muslin of her gown. Chartreuse, Dare thought in an odd non sequitur. He shook his bizarre thoughts about colors from his head, fearing he was losing his mind.

Glancing at his cousin's wife, he inquired, "Do you mind?" She indicated she didn't so he shrugged out of his loose jacket, tossing it halfway across the room to land on the floor under the window.

Dare, perforce, sat on the bed, swinging his feet up and crossing his ankles. He leaned against the headboard, putting his arms up behind his head. He exuded comfortable relaxation. He could almost see the envy on Bri's face.

"Oh, to be a man and able to do whatever one damn well pleases," she sighed, confirming his thoughts.

"I doubt Adam would appreciate you quite so well were you a man," he commented wryly. "And isn't it obvious that even men must deal with the consequences of their actions? I would have thought my example perfect in that regard."

She tipped her head to the side in acknowledgment of his observation.

"I notice you've managed to overcome your anger… for the moment, at least," he remarked. "Kudos to you." He saluted her mockingly with one hand, replacing it behind his head.

His comment succeeded in raising her ire again, although, to her credit, Bri restrained the worst of it.

"You didn't answer my question, Dare," she reminded with dangerous softness.

"I did not," he agreed mildly.

"Are you going to?"

He cocked his head in mock contemplation. "No, I don't think I will. An innocent lady like yourself should not be subjected to such earthy matters as that." His tone was very dry.

Bri snorted. "I will assume from that evasive reply that yes, she was worth all the hell we currently find ourselves in." She shook her head in remonstration. "Selfish, selfish,

Dare."

"Am I to sit through yet another listing of my shortcomings," he asked in all seriousness. "Because Miles has spelled them out most elaborately and I'm not averse to finding other lodgings."

"For your health, that would not be wise," Bri observed prosaically. "Con is sure to take the first opportunity presented to murder you despite Miles's efforts on your behalf. You are probably safer here."

Dare shrugged his shoulders nonchalantly. "If Northwicke succeeds, would it not alleviate many problems? Firmly remove me from… uh, *your* misery?" He chuckled.

"You do not take anything seriously, do you?"

The question sobered him instantly. "Untrue, my dear. I take Jenny very seriously."

The countess brightened. "Indeed?" She paused for a long moment, her eyes intent on his face. "Wonderful. Simply wonderful." She rose to her feet, apparently done haranguing him for the time being.

She moved to his side and leaned close, patting his cheek a trifle sharply. He suspected she wanted to slap him much harder but restrained her impulse.

"Remember to treat her with respect, Dare. I shouldn't

want to kill you. I rather like you. You remind me of me." She straightened and walked to the door. As she passed through the portal, she added, "A very mild, staid version of myself, mind you. But me, nonetheless."

Events proceeded as planned. Jenny stayed in Town long enough to scotch the rumors being spread about her. She and Miles tried to present a happy—or at least a mildly content—front for everyone to see.

Dare, by default, was forced to go along with it. And he hated every second. A fact that, surprisingly enough, was successfully hidden beneath his usual, jocular manner.

He attended parties and routs, danced and flirted, even charmed Lady Guinevere into an occasional smile when he knew she'd have liked nothing better than to have a good cry. Dare stood off to the side—in the ballroom with which he currently graced his presence, and in the life of the person he cared for most in the world.

And it was, honestly, no less than he rightly deserved. He'd not yet had a chance to speak to Jenny privately, a situation that vexed him terribly. He needed to talk to her, find out...

But her brother was like a dog with a bone. The man was never more than a few feet or dancers away from his sister. It was something of a miracle that Dare was even allowed to associate with Gwen. One would have thought they'd guard this daughter with far more vigilance since she was still unattached. Apparently, he was viewed only as a threat to Jenny's peace of mind.

He watched, amused, as Lady Guinevere approached him for the third time that night. If she angled for another dance and he accepted it would cause a mild scandal. It would be tantamount to a proposal. He was feeling self-destructive enough to seriously consider it.

Gwen did not coerce him into standing up with her again. Instead, she begged a favor…ostensibly on her sister's behalf.

"Dare, would you be a dear and fetch me some champagne. All this dancing has made me so thirsty." She fluttered her fan before her as if the cool night air wafting in through the open window behind them was not enough to refresh her.

But, when it benefited him, Dare was a gentlemen. So, bowing politely, he departed on his errand.

He had not taken two steps into the room set aside for refreshments before he realized what was going on. Jenny stood in one corner, nearly hidden behind a potted plant. Her pale blue gown stood out in marked contrast to the leaves that shielded her from view. Apparently, she'd had enough of the ball and had sought out a little peace. Gwen must have known her sister was hiding out there.

He approached her, ignoring the request made of him by Gwen, not caring anymore that he should fetch her something to drink no matter the reason for her entreaty. All he could think about was Jenny, standing isolated in her little corner, already a little bit shunned by the Society she loved…sort of.

"Jenny-love."

Her head lifted from her contemplation of the leafy green plant, blue eyes startled and bewildered. Dare couldn't blame her. He was just as surprised. The endearment had just slipped out. He had meant to be calm, collected, and completely withdrawn in his interrogation of her. Emotions would not aid them in the pickle he'd landed them in.

Ever one to plunge into trouble with both feet, he found himself saying in a near whisper, "You cannot possibly want to marry him, Jenny."

"Why not?" she asked, her tone nonchalant but approaching flippant. "He is as good as any man, I suppose."

"Ha! He is better than most and that's why you can't want him. He would berate you until you either killed him or yourself. Why did you accept him? Surely your father would have given you a choice."

"He did, Dare. I accepted Miles because he cared enough to try to help even though it was not his problem. And part of me hoped…" She paused, swallowing with difficulty. "Part of me hoped that something would happen to change everything."

Like his return.

It was an unspoken thought between them, something they both knew and were equally unwilling to voice.

It stunned him that she'd commit herself to another man, his brother, no less, just to make him come back.

He took another step closer. They were now a mere six inches or so away. He wanted very much to drag her forward, into his arms, but the scandal would surpass anything they'd done to date. Embracing in a public forum? The two gossips just on the other side of the vast room would eat out on that for weeks.

"Jenny, you can't do this. To yourself or Miles. He's so bloody noble. He won't back out so you have to."

She gazed up at him, blue eyes guileless but pensive.

"What are you saying, Dare?"

Another step closer. He was almost touching her with the leaves of the plant still between them. "If you marry him, you'll be miserable. Break the betrothal, Jenny-love."

Jenny inwardly sighed. He wanted her to jilt his brother but he said nothing about taking his place. As much as she would love to tell Miles it was over, she had come to realize that her life and the baby's would be much easier with a husband and father.

"I can't break the engagement, Dare. I've caused my family too much pain already."

"A broken betrothal is tame in comparison."

"Yes, but added to the rest of my sins, it just makes everything worse."

"Were you ever going to tell me?" he asked suddenly, his voice uncolored, bored even.

She sensed the hurt, deep down, and knew he referred to the precious child she carried beneath her heart. It was not an appropriate time to discuss it, but she had seen how her brother made sure they were never alone and supposed it was probably going to be the only time to talk about it.

"It is a waltz. Dance with me, Dare. We can speak more freely there."

"And your brother? Will he murder me for daring to

speak to you?"

"He is tired of scandal. He will not cause a scene." She sounded more confident than she felt. Con hated scandal, true, but he was obsessively protective when it came to his sisters so she couldn't actually be sure that he'd do nothing.

Dare offered his arm. Jenny placed her fingertips on the dark cloth of his jacket, trying not to notice the firmly muscled flesh beneath.

Memories of their lovemaking assailed her and she wanted nothing more than to drag him off to some deserted room and show him just how much she had missed him.

The force of her desire shocked her. For several seconds, she couldn't move. Dare glanced down at her, dark brows furrowed in concern.

"All you all right? You look a little flushed."

Forcing a smile to her lips, she nodded. "I am quite all right. Just a little overheated." She almost laughed at her little private jest.

He gave her a look that said he doubted that and firmly led her back to the ballroom.

Taking her hand in his and placing his other at her waist, he pulled her closer than was strictly proper. He didn't care. As he moved them around the floor, he gazed down at her, stunned at the feelings coursing through his body.

She was as he remembered and yet completely different. His memories were pale in comparison. Her scent, wildflowers and jasmine, was even more subtly alluring than before. Her face was classically beautiful as always but her body had filled out a bit, her breasts straining against the fabric of her gown. He had little doubt it was due to her pregnancy.

Her eyes lifted to meet his and he knew she could plainly see his desire in his eyes. Her own flashed and darkened. He was only mildly surprised when she pulled them even closer. His body tightened in response to her blatant hunger.

This was wrong. No matter how much he viewed her as his, she was engaged to his brother. If they did anything to further the scandal surrounding them, it would bring more shame to Miles, something that man did not deserve.

Striving for sanity when all he really wanted was to do strip her of her clothing and make love to her right there, he brought to mind the subject that upset him most.

"Were you going to tell me? Or were you going to make me wait and count the months after your wedding?"

Jenny blinked up at him, confused in the face of his sudden anger. Her own ignited when she realized exactly what he was accusing her of.

"How dare you? You left me right after... you left me!" she snapped, not bothering to hide her annoyance behind a social smile. "You told no one where you were bound or how to contact you. I'd have told you right away were you here to be told, you insensitive clod. Ooooh!" With that, she turned her head away from his intense scrutiny and emitted what he was quite sure was a growl.

Dare almost grinned. He probably would have if he hadn't at that moment noticed Lord Connor making a beeline for his sister. It was apparent that he would risk scandal to see her kept from distress.

"You were wrong," he remarked casually, moving them adroitly away from Lord Connor and between more dancing couples. He then danced right out of the room and out onto a long terrace where he promptly released her.

Jenny was shocked almost speechless to find herself suddenly outside and standing alone. She gave Dare a look of indignation. "I was wrong?" she asked quietly, too quietly.

He pointed back into the ballroom. "About your brother. He was coming to take you from the floor."

She glanced behind her and stretched up on her toes to see over the heads blocking her vision. Sure enough, a brief parting in the swirling dancers showed Connor gazing around with singular purpose.

"Maybe he searches for Gwen." Her tone did not indicate that she believed her own suggestion.

"Perhaps," Dare allowed. "She is off with my brother somewhere, after all."

Jenny's astonished eyes returned to her companion. "What?" Her hands clenched and unclenched at her sides, testament of her continued irritation.

Dare leaned back against the stone balustrade, crossing his arms over his chest. "I saw them leave as we began to waltz. Perhaps they hoped everyone would believe we were them and not realize that it was the *good* couple who went off to...*talk*."

"Are you implying that they are...What are you implying?"

Dare moved from his relaxed pose and leaned forward, brushing her cheek playfully. "Come, Jenny-love, you are not so innocent anymore. What do you think I imply?"

"You are no gentleman to bring that so plainly to my attention," she complained.

He smiled and resumed his pose. "What? The implication that my brother is making love to your sister? Or that you are no longer innocent?"

"Either. Neither. Both. Oh, I don't know!"

Jenny turned abruptly away. She was fast approaching that point where she reacted without thought. If they continued to talk this way she just might strike him.

Or kiss him. Which would be worse?

Placing her hands on the balustrade, she took several deep breaths, trying desperately to calm herself.

She wasn't aware of Dare's having moved until he stood right behind her. His arms came around her to rest on the stone next to hers, effectively pressing his front all along her back. A shiver wracked her suddenly and she couldn't stop herself from pressing back into him, relishing the warmth and hardness of his body.

"Does it bother you so much then?" he asked, breathing the words softly in her ear. He lightly nipped her lobe. She shivered again and closed her eyes, feeling his erotic caress throughout her entire frame.

"What?" she asked, aware of a strange huskiness in her voice.

"Miles," he told her, pressing his lips to that sensitive spot just below her ear. A soft moan escaped her. "And Gwen."

Is that what he thought? That she would be upset about her betrothed and her sister, two people who'd had feelings for each other since the first moment they'd met?

"No. I wish them well," she managed to murmur as his lips moved down her neck and around her throat. "I wish them"—pausing on a moan as his tongue ran over the smooth skin of her shoulder—"all the pleasure"—another moan as he turned her in his arms—"they can steal."

Finally, finally, Dare kissed her. It was not a sweet meeting of mouths but rather something far more primitive. An explosion of hunger erupted between them, making them lose sense of place and time. All their pent-up emotions, the anger, betrayal, desolation, and loss was communicated in their embrace. It was as if they were trying to store up whatever memories they could before their inevitable parting.

Her hands found their way into his hair, removing the riband securing the long black strands. A sensual shiver raced down her spine at the feel of the silky locks slipping through her fingers. She loved his hair. It was the first thing that attracted her during their first meeting.

He was trailing kisses all along the swell of her breasts when she heard the unmistakable sound of a throat being cleared. Her head shot up, nearly colliding with Dare's.

It was her father.

She groaned and tried to step away from her lover.

Dare's arms tightened, however, preventing her retreat. She looked at him, her eyes wide and pleading. He looked obstinately back at her.

"As much as I hate to interrupt this...ah, *touching* moment," the duke drawled with deceptive calm, "I'm afraid I must ask you to release my daughter."

"And if I don't?" Dare had the temerity to inquire, meeting Lord Denbigh's gaze steadily. They both knew he wasn't merely speaking of that particular moment in time.

The duke stared sedately at him. "I am too old to make threats, young man. I will allow that this incident was a bout of moon-madness and pretend nothing happened. Should it occur again, however, I will have to kill you."

The last was said with such calm finality that Dare felt Jenny shiver and just barely restrained a shiver of his own. With more regret than he could fully hide, he dropped his arms.

Jenny took one step away from him but, to her credit, did not cower before her father. She lifted her chin, a tiny, secretive smile playing about her kiss-swollen lips.

"Come, Jenny. We must leave. Gwen departed some time ago under Miles's escort due to a headache. We should not tarry too long in our own departure."

"Yes, Father," she murmured dutifully.

As she moved past Dare, Jenny met his dark eyes, her own laughing mischievously. There was something she wasn't telling him. And he was very worried that whatever it was would probably plunge them all into far more scandal than he ever could have dreamed.

Dare was right.

The following morning Adam entered his wife's drawing room and bluntly announced:

"Gwen has eloped. With Miles."

Fourteen

"Miles would never do such a thing," stated that young man's twin with rigid finality.

Adam shrugged helplessly. "And yet he has. Denbigh and Con are breathing fire and for some reason, their animosity is directed at you."

Dare snorted. "As is ever the function of the black sheep."

"Unfortunately, that is often the case." The older man sat down and leaned back in his chair, studying his cousin intently. "You realize, of course, that this leaves Jenny with a huge problem and no husband to show for it."

Dare started. It was true. And more than he could comfortably take in at the moment.

"I think it would be in everyone's best interest if you were to offer for the girl."

Dare looked up from his clenched fists. "Would she have me?"

"I very much doubt her father will give her a choice.

Who would have her now, nearly three months gone with another man's child?"

"Blunt, but true," Dare drawled. "And as I am the father, one would assume I have at least half a chance of securing her hand." He shrugged.

Adam watched him impassively. Bri was unaccountably silent. Dare glanced over at her to see her smiling. His heart stopped. She wore the same expression Jenny had worn the night before, mischievous and secretive.

Adam noticed the direction of Dare's gaze and looked at his wife as well. His eyes narrowed suspiciously. "What have you done, madam?"

Bri started guiltily. Then, as usual, her natural—or perhaps unnatural—defiance reared up. "Nothing that didn't need to be done, Adam Prestwich. And don't you dare give me that look. I don't deserve to be punished. I have done nothing—!"

Her excuses ended on an indignant squeal as Adam lifted her from her chair. "What—have—you—done?" he bit out harshly.

Dare leapt to his feet, knowing it was unwise to get in the middle of a domestic argument, but reconciling his interference with the irrefutable truth that this particular argument stemmed from something that directly concerned himself and so was partially his fault.

Grabbing his cousin's arm, he urged, "Adam, she's carrying your child. Release her before you do damage to it."

His words were instantly heeded. Adam had not actually done anything more than grip her hard, just enough to let her know he was in earnest. He stepped away now, his irritation a palpable entity in the room.

Dare sighed in relief. He knew Adam would never hurt Bri but with all the tension over all the stupid actions being committed left and right in this farce, Dare wasn't sure Adam had a very good hold on his roiling displeasure.

Helping Bri back to her seat, he warned in an undertone, "I am not above letting him shake you, Bri, so please do not anger either one of us further. What have you and Jenny done and who helped you do it?"

She remained mulishly silent for a moment, her gaze locked on her husband's rigid back. Then, as Dare's words penetrated, she glanced quickly up at him, her eyes revealing her shock at how perceptive he was.

Dare straightened, throwing a sharp look at Adam. He was not naïve enough to believe Adam had not heard every word he'd uttered to his lady wife. He was also quite aware that he couldn't stop Adam a second time should the older man decide to punish his willful wife.

"Talk," Adam commanded, his back still turned to them.

Bri released a feral sound from deep in her throat. "Gwen asked for my help. She knew Jenny would be miserable with Miles so she wanted to break the engagement."

"How did you get Miles to agree?" Adam asked.

Dare answered, his gaze glued to Bri's obstinately beautiful face. "They didn't."

Bri's face revealed the truth of Dare's statement.

Adam's face suffused with color. "What the bloody hell does that mean?"

Dare turned laughing eyes to his cousin. "Miles has not eloped, Adam. He's been kidnapped."

Adam's face reflected astonishment for a moment before he and Dare burst into uncontrollable laughter. Bri turned shocked eyes from one man to the other.

Dare wiped tears from his eyes and slumped down onto the settee beside Lady Prestwich. He slouched down, covering his eyes with one hand, his body still shaking with silent laughter.

Adam was not faring much better. He still stood, but

barely. He leaned heavily on the mantle, his shoulders shaking. Every once in a while, a snort escaped him, making Bri stare in wonder.

It wasn't long before she got very annoyed. "Are the two of you quite through?"

Dare nodded, his face wet with tears, his body still rhythmically shaking. Adam waved a hand in her direction but did not look at her or say a word.

Both gentlemen made every effort to compose themselves It was a few moments later that they finally succeeded.

Lady Prestwich sat, arms folded over her chest, glaring at one man and then the other, over and over. Dare apologized prettily, winning a reluctant smile from her. Adam snorted at his cousin's gesture and merely bowed to his wife, a chuckle or two escaping.

"Would one of you mind explaining that."

Adam chose to answer. "Darling, you know Miles. Can you imagine his outrage and horror when he was informed of their destination? Not the stuff of a young maiden's dreams, I assure you."

Bri chuckled a bit then, her imagination allowing her to conjure the picture Adam painted. "Ah, yes. It was cruel to do that to him, was it not?"

Adam's jocularity abruptly dissipated. "Do you realize just what it is you've done, woman?"

She bristled. "I have cleared the way for Dare and Jenny."

Dare's eyes threatened to pop out of his head. He sat up, staring at her in utter shock. "You have cleared the way for me and Jenny?" he asked numbly. "What right did you have to meddle?"

The lady's cheeks bloomed pink. "I thought I was helping. Gwen assured me that Miles loves her and you love Jenny."

"Gwen assured you? And that's another thing. This doesn't sound like Gwen. This sounds more like… damnation! It was Jenny and you. Gwen had nothing to do with it."

Adam muttered a few choice oaths at Dare's realization and his wife's headstrong interference. "Denbigh will have all our hides for this, make no mistake."

Dare groaned. He flopped back and threw an arm dramatically over his eyes. "I am lost," he muttered. "What shall I do now? My brother is gone. His betrothed waits in vain for him."

Bri punched him. And it was no frail action, either.

Dare laughed even as he yelped in sudden pain.

"Good God, woman! Do you realize the damage you could have done had you aimed lower?" His laughter took the sting out of his words but Bri continued to glare at him anyway.

"I should have struck you there, you ignorant clod."

"That's twice in the four-and-twenty hours I've been called a clod," he mused to Adam. "Could there be truth in it, do you think?"

Adam grunted. "Undoubtedly."

Dare's face split into a wide grin as if something momentous had just occurred. And perhaps it had.

"Do you suppose Miles will be less uptight after this?" he asked his companions, truly delighted with the idea.

Adam ignored him. "Who actually kidnapped them, Bri?"

She looked away and mumbled something indistinct. Adam emitted a low sound of warning. Bri's head shot up defiantly and she snapped, "Vi! Levi agreed to do it. Viewed it as quite a lark, in fact, eager as he was to bring Miles down from his lofty pedestal."

"Levi? Lord Greville?"

Adam nodded to Dare. "Bri's incredibly dull-witted cousin, Levi, Lord Greville. Ever will that sapskull be a thorn in my side."

"Oh, Bri, you may have actually created a scandal to overshadow mine."

"Perhaps I have, Dare. But there is something you should know. Jenny had nothing to do with it. Gwen finally took matters into her own hands."

Lord Connor Northwicke was seen by several acquaintances marching into Lockwood House in the devil of a temper. It was speculated that he was there to do murder but who would be his victim was in question.

Many assumed Mr. Darius Prestwich was the one Lord Connor sought. And yet, it was Mr. Miles who had done the unthinkable and eloped with Lady Guinevere. But, since Miles was *in absentia*, it was speculated that perhaps the young lord was there intent on murdering his lifelong friend, Sir Adam.

Adam received Connor in his study, mentally sighing. It was not an interview he anticipated with any sort of eagerness. All he felt was resignation and his own desire to do his two young cousins an injury.

Lord Connor sat, his face arranged in lines of

disappointed anger. Adam reclined in his chair, his own face revealing nothing of his feelings, as usual.

"I do not hold you responsible in any way, Adam," Connor told him quietly. "They are grown men, after all, and should know better how to behave."

Adam's lips twisted into a mocking smile. "Ah, yes. Grown men." He picked up a quill from his desk and stared at it, his eyes unfocused and his mind rebelling from what he had to tell his best friend.

"Actually, Con, it is my fault," he said, glancing up as he tossed the pen back on the desk.

Lord Connor's surprise was writ plain in his expression "You forced Dare to seduce Jenny? Or do you speak of the elopement?"

Adam sighed. "The elopement. Apparently, Miles had nothing to do with it. Gwen planned it all… with Bri's help."

Connor nodded. "I see. Would chasing them down do any good, do you think?"

Adam shook his head. "Miles will marry her and perhaps it would be best at this point. If she returns unmarried still, her reputation will be less than Jenny's. And knowing Miles as I do, he will not let that happen."

"I thought as much," Connor admitted. "I just don't

understand why they could not have approached my father, as is proper, and asked for their hands."

"Would he have listened? Two young men, one with a blackened past, neither with very deep pockets, neither in possession of a title, asking for the hands of the daughters of the Duke of Denbigh? I admit that I understand why they did not even bother."

"That's a little unfair of you, Adam," Connor remonstrated. "We are not so shallow as that."

"What have you to do with it, Con? Would it not have been your father's decision?"

His friend's seeming hostility nonplussed Connor. But then, this was Adam's family they discussed and he could understand protective bonds of familial devotion.

But it was Connor's sisters who were ruined by the Prestwich men. That was something that gave Connor the right to feel any damn way that he pleased.

"This discussion will accomplish nothing but hard feelings between the two of us, the two in the whole situation with the least power," Adam inserted calmly. "Has Denbigh decided what he will do about Jenny?"

"He wants Dare to marry her," Connor revealed without preamble. "Jenny has agreed. Seemed almost pleased, in fact, although I think it may be simple relief that her child will not suffer the ignominy of bastardy."

Adam kept his thoughts on that nonsensical assumption to himself. He had never known Connor to be so dense before but perhaps his concern for his sisters blinded him to what was obvious.

Connor rose. "Have Dare come round tomorrow afternoon. Father will inform him of his options then."

Adam nodded, watching Lord Connor leave. Something in the other man's manner was not right. Adam had a feeling Dare was not going to like Denbigh's proposition.

Fifteen

"I have a proposition for you, young man."

Dare eyed Lord Denbigh warily. He wouldn't have been surprised if the man suggested Dare take a long walk off a short pier. Indeed, he wouldn't have blamed him.

"Indeed," was all he said in reply, completely devoid of emotion.

"As you are the reason my daughter finds herself in this... untenable position, it seems only fair that you make it right."

Dare hardly dared hope. Was the duke actually suggesting he marry Jenny? Could his life actually turn out so well?

"In what way, your grace?"

The Duke of Denbigh gave him a long, considering look. "You will marry her, of course. Is there any other way?"

Dare released a breath he'd not realized he was holding. It took every ounce of his willpower to stifle the shout of joy that welled up inside him. "Indeed not. Of course I shall marry her," he managed to say blandly.

The duke fingered the quill he held, solemnly regarding the young man before him. "You will not receive the dowry I had thought to settle on her. She will be given an annuity from her grandmother's legacy that will allow her to live in modest comfort, but she will retain power over her own funds."

Although offended, Dare didn't show it. "I expected nothing less," he admitted in the same bland, almost bored tone.

And it was true. It made sense that they would assume he was a fortune hunter and Dare hadn't seen fit to inform anybody otherwise. Not even Adam knew exactly how much he was worth. He almost wished he could see the duke's face when it became common knowledge.

"Time is of the essence. To that end, you will be married in two days. Immediately following the ceremony, you will depart. Jenny will remain here with her family."

Dare was almost too shocked to reply. After a moment, he asked a trifle shortly, "Where am I going?"

The duke waved a hand imperiously. "I neither know nor do I care. You are to make yourself scarce."

"Why...the bloody *hell*...would I do that?" Dare bit

off each word, angered beyond bearing.

Denbigh sent him a look of disgust. "You are not worthy of my daughter, sir. I will not have her made miserable by the fact that she married so far beneath her."

Dare snorted in disbelief. He just couldn't help it. "So far beneath her? I am the son of a gentleman, your grace. Our stations are not that dissimilar."

"But you are a scoundrel. And while necessity requires that Jenny be married, and quickly, she does not have to have a daily reminder of how low she's sunk."

Their discussion could quickly escalate into a shouting match. Dare didn't let that faze him. While he held himself primarily to blame for the whole situation, he was practical enough to allow Jenny some responsibility as well. It hadn't been rape, after all.

He couldn't keep a trace of sarcasm from coloring his reply. "I would think she'd have that anyway, when the child arrives."

A spasm of pain nearly made Dare clutch at his heart. His child. Would he never get to see his own baby? A sweet little being with blond hair and cornflower eyes just like its mother.

"At least the child will be legitimate. And she has already shown that she eagerly awaits the child's birth."

That, at least, gave Dare some small comfort. A woman who so looked forward to her child's arrival couldn't totally hate the man who gave it to her...could she?

"Is Jenny aware of your...plans?"

"Yes."

The single word, said without hesitation, would have brought Dare to his knees had he been standing. He was thankful he was not. He couldn't appear so weak before this man.

After a moment of intense concentration, he forced his body up. He took a deep breath, tamping down his anger and dismay. "Very well. I will return in two days. Good day, your grace."

Dare wondered ever after how he'd actually managed to walk out. He entered Adam's carriage, his extremities numb to the drizzle in the air.

He would not weep. Yelling with more force than necessary, he ordered the coachman to drop him at the nearest tavern, the lower the company, the better. Once there, Dare proceeded to get very, very drunk.

They were duly married. Jenny said her vows in hardly more than a whisper. Dare's were a little louder but with an air of boredom that was quite insulting to the bride and her family.

The groom didn't care. He wanted to be anywhere but where he was. He had wanted this woman from the first moment he saw her, and now that he finally had her, he was being forced to leave her…again.

The cleric finished with more joy than was being displayed by anyone else. He suggested the groom kiss the bride and then stood there and beamed at them, completely oblivious to the undercurrents of misery, resignation, and anger that were a nearly palpable entity in the small saloon.

Glancing down at Jenny, he saw she was watching him, but not with anger, more like despair.

Her misery enraged him. A few short months ago, Dare would have been the first to say she had reason, being trapped into marriage with him. But now, she had no need to be miserable, as he would be leaving before the ink was dry on the marriage lines.

Something perverse nudged Dare. Snaking an arm around her waist, he brought her up against him, hard. Not a breath of air could pass between them from chest to thigh. He knew she could feel the proof of his hunger for her. Lips parting on a soft gasp, her eyes darkened with desire.

Dare kissed her brutally, without honor or respect, branding her, marking her. He wanted her under no delusions about his possession of her.

There was a collective gasp from their astonished audience. Dare broke the kiss before anyone could forcefully remove him from the room.

Looking deep into lambent blue eyes, the bridegroom growled, "Remember that while I'm gone."

Abruptly releasing her, he stalked from the room.

Jenny was too astonished to do more than watch him go. Then, suddenly, her knees gave out and she crumpled to the floor, tears coursing down her pale cheeks. Burying her face in her hands, she wept, releasing all the tears she'd held back.

Her mother's arms came around her but she was too distraught to take any comfort from the gesture. Her life was ruined and she was unsure exactly who to blame.

"Shh, love. Calm yourself. Think of the child."

Her mother's softly whispered plea penetrated her hysterical sobs. Straightening from her near-fetal position on the floor, Jenny swiped at the seemingly endless flow of tears.

Gulping rather inelegantly, she managed to say around the huge lump in her throat, "He left. How could he leave?"

The duchess's eyes glistened with sympathetic moisture. "Oh, my poor dear. You love that man." It was not a question, but rather a startling realization on the part of a parent determined to do the right thing for her child no matter how distasteful the action might seem.

And distasteful it had been. Lady Denbigh had not agreed with her husband's decision to force Darius Prestwich to leave but she had supported him because she thought her daughter might be better off with an absent husband.

But now, after the groom had so angrily stormed off to only God knows where, the Duchess of Denbigh realized how very wrong they'd been. Jenny loved the man, no matter how many mistakes he'd made. And if her suspicions were correct, Lady Denbigh was quite sure Dare loved her daughter with equal force.

Looking up, the duchess met her husband's angered blue eyes. She couldn't prevent a tear from falling. The duke stood stoically, for all intents and purposes unaffected by the whole debacle.

But she knew her husband. He was hurting as much as she was; indeed, more so. He was simply better at hiding it.

Connor, on the other hand, usually very adept at hiding his feelings, looked ready to do murder.

Something in the duchess snapped. Her baby was hurting and her men were standing there doing nothing to help.

"Go after him, you fools," she hissed. It was something so unlike her usual calm poise that they stared at her as if seeing her for the first time.

Shaking off the perverse spurt of satisfaction she felt at managing to shock them—they were two men who did not shock easily—she added, "You have to catch him. If he leaves he may never return because his pride won't let him. If he doesn't return..." She let her words trail meaningfully to a halt, hoping she wouldn't have to spell it out for them in front of Jenny, who Lady Denbigh knew was listening despite her tears.

Connor's bright eyes fell on his sister, reading her posture and actions with the senses of a bloodhound. He glanced up at his father, sharing the briefest of looks before he turned and ran from the room.

They waited.

And waited.

Jenny managed to bring her raging emotions under control, for the baby's sake if no one else's. It was apparent, to her at least, that this child was all she'd have of the man she loved more than life itself.

Connor finally returned, his facial features drawn into a mighty frown. He stopped abruptly in the doorway, sought out Jenny's red-rimmed eyes, and sighed, shaking his head.

Jenny bit her lower lip, determined not to dissolve again. It was as she'd suspected—he was gone.

Standing with regal dignity, Lady Genevieve Prestwich nodded once to her brother, curtsied to her father, and turned to her mother. Imbuing her words with a measure of haughty disdain, she said, "I'd like to leave."

Her request startled everyone. It had been planned that Jenny would stay with her family, just as if nothing had changed. She knew this but had been led to believe that while Dare had certain obligations he could not ignore, she would see him from time to time whenever he returned to England. She had not been informed that part of her father's plans were to deny Jenny her husband.

It was all so clear now. Dare hadn't left because he wanted to. He'd been compelled to leave.

When no one responded to her demand, she raised one

brow in haughty inquiry. "I assume there is a small house somewhere that can be leased for me." Sending a sidelong glance of scorn in her brother's direction, she added, "I will not stay here. I *refuse* to stay with people who care so little for me."

The duke was stunned but retained enough presence of mind to say, softly, "Everything we've done was out of love for you, Jenny."

"Love for me?" she scoffed, every rigid inch of her body speaking of her icy contempt for their *loving* attention. "You speak of love for me." She drew in a shuddery breath. "Your *love*," she said, making the word sound abhorrent. "Your love for me has cost me a husband. A man worth the lot of you put together. In character if not in property. But, apparently, property is what's important to you. So, I will assume that a place will be provided for me. It is the least you can do, considering."

She swept from the room, drawing her primrose skirts around her, lest they brush her brother's legs as she left. She did not miss the look of hurt in Con's eyes, and though it pained her to do something so despicable to the brother she had loved so well, she resolutely ignored it.

Sixteen

Her father did not disappoint her in his choice of residence. He provided her with a quaint little cottage nearly fifteen miles away from her family home. It was far enough that she could ignore them but close enough that those in the vicinity could still feel the duke's power.

Jenny settled in quickly, determined to make a life for herself and her baby. She hoped and prayed her husband would one day return, even knowing that the chances of such an occurrence were slim indeed.

Her father provided a maid-of-all-work and a cook, plus a man to do the outside work and any heavy lifting and such. The maid lived in while the cook and manservant came for the day and went home to their own families at night.

The maid, Lucy, was a pleasant, youngish woman, much of an age with Jenny. A part of her wondered if perhaps her father was trying to provide her with a friend in the understanding, bubbly girl. But, as it wasn't important to her, she didn't dwell on it overlong.

It also occurred to her that Lucy was, in actuality, a spy for her father. She didn't care. Lucy could tell them whatever she chose to impart. It would not change Jenny's feelings toward her family and their meddling.

Jenny filled her days with sewing little infant garments for her baby, whose arrival was even more anxiously awaited than before. Her days she could fill with mindless, thoughtless activities.

That was simple.

But her nights...her nights were spent regretting the loss of her husband and reliving the one intimate encounter she'd had with him. What she wouldn't give for just one night in his arms!

She'd wake every morning with tears dried on her face, miserably sad.

And her family avoided her.

After the first few weeks of refusing to see any of them, they stopped coming, only sending the occasional note. She never read the notes unless they came from her mother and even then, she never answered them.

Gwen had returned from Scotland with her new husband and been accepted back into the family fold. Even Miles, despite his having run off with the precious Lady

Guinevere Northwicke, was wholeheartedly accepted. It was just one more thing to add to her already immense bitterness towards her family.

She had no way of knowing it was their conduct with Dare that made them more willing to accept Miles, in spite of his actions—actions of which Jenny still had no real knowledge.

It was with a great amount of willpower that Jenny refused to see her twin when Gwen showed up on her doorstep.

Things might have gone on in this less than healthy vein for quite some time had not Jenny received a surprise and wholly unexpected visitor.

She was due to have her child sometime within the next month. She was ungainly, and so large that she was positive she was carrying twins.

It would not be surprising, she thought wryly, a sad twisting of her lips passing for a smile.

She was walking in the garden, enjoying the mild fall weather when she was alerted to the sound of a horse approaching. She circled around the house to the front door, her steps slow and ponderous.

She heard the visitor dismount before she'd quite reached the front. When she finally rounded the last corner, she looked up.

And gasped.

Dare?

A second, closer look revealed that it wasn't, in fact, *her* husband but her sister's. Dare's eyes were just a shade darker, his hair a touch longer.

And he was far handsomer, in Jenny's biased opinion.

Knowing she actually had it in her to be quite rude to an unwelcome guest—she'd more than proven that these past few months—she also knew there was no way she could turn away her husband's twin brother.

So, pasting on a determined smile, she advanced, holding out one hand while holding her skirts with the other.

"Miles, how lovely to see you," she lied.

Miles looked her over carefully, as if searching for visible injuries. Finally, he met her eyes. "You look radiant, Jenny," he told her softly.

She released a rather unladylike snort. "Nonsense. I am a cow and look as tired as I feel." Hoping rather perversely that he would decline, she asked, "Would you care for tea?"

He accepted after another drawn out moment of careful thought. Jenny reflected that Miles hadn't changed at all, even after doing something so unexpected like eloping with her sister. He still made every decision only after careful thought.

"How is Gwen?" she asked, leading the way into the cottage.

"She would be much better if you'd agree to see her," was his acerbic reply.

Jenny turned, meeting Miles's eyes with both of her pale brows lifted in surprise. Perhaps he had changed some after all. She was absurdly pleased.

"I am rather…estranged from my family, as you surely know," she said in response.

"I can understand that, having been filled in on some horrifying details before I was pressed into coming to see you. I fail to see, however, how that affects your relationship with your twin. She'd never hurt you."

Jenny gestured toward one of the two comfortable armchairs in her quaint little sitting room. She moved to the bellpull but Miles beat her there, giving it a tug before helping her to her own seat, opposite his.

She smiled her thanks even as she remarked, "I know she never meant to hurt me, Miles. And part of me, despite how everything has turned out, is grateful that she stole you from me. But another part of me can't get past the fact that I could be contentedly married to you instead of miserably married to your brother."

A moment of stunned silence followed. "That was blunt," her guest finally said, a bit woodenly. "I'm not sure how to respond to that."

Jenny shrugged and would have replied but Lucy walked in, bobbed a curtsy, and asked what she could do. Jenny smiled with genuine affection at the maid and ordered tea.

When she'd gone, Jenny said, "It has all worked out for the best though."

This time, it was Miles who snorted. "That is highly debatable."

Her smile wavered a bit. "Perhaps it is," she admitted readily. "It would be far better had Dare stayed despite whatever my father told him to induce him to leave." A tear trembled on her lashes, but she wiped it away briskly. "None of it matters anymore anyway. For all we know, he's dead."

Her statement ended on a rather strangled note and she had to duck her head to hide the sudden welling in her eyes. She would not cry now. Not after so many months... or weeks… very well, days without shedding a tear.

Hours, rather, she thought dejectedly.

Miles moved across the room, knelt at her feet. She hadn't even realized he'd gotten up until he lifted her chin.

"He is not dead, Jenny. He writes Adam faithfully every week."

An inarticulate "Oh" was all she managed to say to that little piece of information. "How is he?" She tried not to sound too terribly interested but even her child must have sensed her tension. A strong kick was her answer from that quarter.

Miles must have felt it, close as he was to her. His eyes widened and he smiled for the first time since arriving.

Impulsively, Jenny took his hand and placed it on her distended belly. She might not be able to share this wonderful part of pregnancy with her husband but she hoped he could at least experience some of it through the bond he shared with his twin if nothing else.

Miles resisted the improper gesture at first but then he relaxed and pressed his palm gently against her stomach.

As they waited for the next movement, he murmured, "He asks Adam and Bri about you." A tiny flutter under his palm coincided with her swift intake of breath. He smiled sadly, glancing up at his sister-in-law. "He misses you and constantly asks about his child." Another flutter, stronger this time. Miles almost thought the baby was reacting to his voice if not his actual words.

Carefully meeting her eyes, he demanded gently but firmly, "Answer a question for me, Jenny." She nodded, her hand still clasped over his on her belly. "If Dare returned, would you accept him?"

Jenny's quivering chin heralded the onslaught of another bout of weeping. Nodding emphatically, she whispered, "I accepted him long ago, Miles. I would have told him at our wedding if he had but given me the chance."

The baby—or babies—settled down, apparently having managed to wear itself out. Miles returned to his seat, a thoughtful smile playing about his lips.

Jenny, painfully aware of just how alike Miles and her husband were, stifled the urge to demand Miles's swift departure. It was most depressing to gaze at the mirror image of the man with whom she was in love. Especially when she grew more and more sure with each passing day that her husband would not return.

Holding the incipient tears firmly in abeyance, she asked, "Why did my family send you to me?" Lifting the teapot, she poured some into two cups and, without thinking, added a dollop of cream to one, handing it to her guest.

Miles stared at her blankly. Having had tea several times with Jenny and Gwen in the months that he'd known them, he knew that Jenny was fully aware of how he liked his tea—sugar, no cream.

Dare preferred his with cream, no sugar…when whiskey wasn't available, that is.

Miles wondered uneasily if he might break down and cry himself before this visit was over.

Jenny, after a moment of protracted silence, met Miles's eyes in confusion. He just sat there, holding his teacup, glancing at it oddly. Then she realized what she'd done.

Using the very last of her reserve of strength, Jenny forced a laugh from her achingly tight throat. "Oh, dear," she murmured. Spooning sugar into her own tea, she handed it across to him. "I am sorry, Miles. I wasn't thinking." Her voice trailed away on a broken little sob and she fell silent.

Miles shook his head. "Please do not distress yourself, Jenny." He paused, then set aside the tea he held, leaning forward slightly. "I was sent to try to convince you to relent towards your family," he admitted.

A lengthy pause followed in which Jenny waited for him to continue. When he didn't, she asked, "And why haven't you?"

He sighed a little. "I think a part of me is just as upset as you are. Dare, while having behaved rather badly at first, should not be treated as if he is dirt for the rest of his life."

"I did wonder why you were so readily accepted upon your return."

"Denbigh admitted he was wrong."

Something inside Jenny clenched. "He actually said that?" she managed to whisper around the pain tightening around her heart.

Miles nodded. "Con did as well."

The tears could not longer be held back. Jenny cried. And cried. And cried.

Miles watched helplessly, not sure what he could do to help but knowing he should do something.

In the end, he just waited for her to compose herself.

Jenny did, finally, bring her tears under control. She started to laugh then, odd, tearful sort of sounds that bordered on the hysterical. Miles was confused and alarmed by her behavior.

"Is that supposed to make everything all right now?" she asked sharply, each word punctuated by another choking sound of mirthless laughter. "Am I supposed to skip back home now, content and at ease, because Daddy and Con admitted they were wrong?" Her voice was approaching shrill but the laughter had stopped, replaced by fury. "I have a problem with that logic, Miles Prestwich. They may have been wrong, but I still have NO HUSBAND!"

Miles rose and grasped her by the arms, bringing her up to her feet. Giving her the tiniest of shakes, he snapped angrily, "Actually, Jenny, no one assumed anything. You've proven beyond doubt these months past that you cannot forgive. Even the sister to whom you owe much."

He suddenly dropped his hands as if burned, stepping back a few paces to avoid doing something despicable like strike the infuriating little witch.

Jenny stared at him wide-eyed. "What do I owe her?" she asked softly, truly curious as to his answer.

Miles sighed deeply, splaying the fingers of his right hand through his short black hair. "It was Gwen who wanted to elope, Jenny," he confessed. "She tried to convince me it was the only way to make sure you were able to wed Dare. She knew your father would convince Dare to do right by you if he didn't come to the decision on his own."

"And, obviously, you agreed."

"I didn't," he admitted. He stared at her a long moments as if unsure whether to continue. Finally, he added, "Gwen asked Lady Prestwich for help who in turn asked Lord Greville for help. Greville kidnapped me and it wasn't until I woke up in Gwen's bed that I was informed that we were eloping." His expression mirrored his self-disgust. "I had no choice but to continue on to Gretna."

"You could have returned and let Gwen deal with her own ruined reputation," Jenny pointed out, knowing Miles would never have done such a thing in a million years.

"I could have," he surprised her by admitting. "And I would have, considering how extremely improper, not to mention dangerous, her actions were, had I not already been completely in love with her."

Jenny smiled sincerely and truly at her unwanted guest. "I knew. Had Gwen asked me to help I would have."

Miles dipped his head in acknowledgment of her rather backhanded compliment. "Gwen managed to convince me that it was for the best anyway. But I swear, neither of us even suspected Denbigh would make Dare leave after the vows."

"I do not blame you, Miles, or Gwen. I am glad at least, of the four of us, that two are happy with how their lives have ended up." Smoothing her hands over her belly,

Jenny gazed down unseeingly. With a difficult little breath, she met his eyes again. "I am truly happy for you and my sister. But I cannot let go yet." Her breath caught on a sob. "I have no pride anymore. If Dare showed up right now, I'd beg him to stay, promising anything in my power to induce him. At this point, all I have is my resentment. I have little doubt that I will relent in time."

She paused, gazing off into the distance. "I can't explain it, Miles. It doesn't make sense to me. I feel as though the resentment is all that is holding me together. If I let go, I'll shatter."

It was a very thoughtful Miles Prestwich that left the very pregnant Lady Genevieve moments later. He rode in utter silence, pondering deeply the things she'd revealed… and some things she hadn't.

It was apparent to the veriest nodcock that she was deeply in love with his brother, despite assurances by certain other parties that her feelings were superficial. Had he not seen her tears and heard her assertion from her own lips, he still would have believed she was in love with Dare. It was in her every movement, her every breath.

And she was waiting for her husband to return.

Miles drew in a deep breath. His intuition, not to mention the fact that he could feel his twin's pain, told him that Dare wanted his family. But Miles was unsure if Dare's pride had relented enough to allow him to return.

Other than inquiring after her health in the vaguest of terms, Dare had not mentioned Jenny in any of the many letters he'd sent to Adam. He'd asked about the child, if it had arrived yet and begged—*begged!*—for details about it.

Oh yes, Miles knew Dare wanted the baby. But pride was a damnably hard thing to discard.

Seventeen

Some months later...

Dare stepped off the boat, experiencing a feeling of intense *déjà vu*. He shivered from more than just the cold, glancing around uneasily, almost expecting to see Adam with a gentleman and a veiled lady. But he could see nothing through the early morning fog.

He was reasonably startled, therefore, when Adam emerged from the mist. In fact, he nearly jumped from his skin.

"Adam! Damn and blast, what the devil are you trying to do? You scared me half to death." He forced his breathing to still, not liking his cousin's grim expression.

But then, Adam always looked grim.

Jenny's face lifted before his mind's eye, her beautiful face creased in delight, laughing at some jest. He choked back a groan. Even after all these months, just picturing her could nearly bring him to his knees.

With Jenny firmly in his thoughts, he asked sharply, "How is she? And the baby?"

Adam put his arm around the younger man's shoulders, leading him firmly in a particular direction. Dare realized with something akin to panic that Adam was far grimmer than was his wont.

"I have a carriage," the baronet told him, pointedly delaying his answer.

Dare considered digging in his heels, forcing his cousin to speak, but realized the futility of such an action. Adam could not be forced. Bri was able to cajole, coerce, or bribe him upon occasion but even she was only able to do what Adam allowed.

So he went with Adam, his mind concocting all kinds of horrific things that could have happened to Jenny and the baby. Fearing madness, he stifled the fears, adopting a bland expression.

Once ensconced in his carriage, Adam asked, "What did you discover? Was it Penryn?"

Dare decided to allow Adam's choice in conversation since there was much on that score he needed to reveal and it was rather imperative that he do so.

So, fears for his wife firmly suppressed, he disclosed, "Penryn was involved but not in the way we suspected."

Adam's eyebrows raised slightly. "Indeed? How was he involved if not in charge?"

"Honestly, he knew nothing about it. It was one of his captains, his most trusted, to be precise."

"Hence, the reason it appeared to be Penryn himself behind it all."

"Exactly. The man has apparently been wrecking for years." Dare leaned forward, warming to his theme. "Nearly a decade ago, the earl's brother was the ringleader, wrecking and causing general mayhem. The brother went to Waterloo and returned a trifle unbalanced. Added to his earlier criminal tendencies, he became a force to be reckoned with. One of Penryn's employees—incidentally, she is now his wife—uncovered a plot to kill Penryn. His brother was killed. Evidently, the captain, being employed by the Earls of Penryn for more than thirty years, took it upon himself to continue with the young honorable's chosen profession, having not been implicated himself."

"What has Penryn done?"

"Had the captain taken up on charges, of course. But the blasted magistrate lost the fellow and a posse had to be assembled." Dare leaned back, a smile of supreme satisfaction crossing his dark features. "I found the blackguard hiding out in a shack on Penryn's own estate."

"You *found* him?"

Dare's expression became shuttered. "He will not be wrecking any more of your ships, I assure you."

Adam let it go at that, satisfied. "And Penryn?"

"Sends his abject apologies and this." Dare handed Adam a small slip of paper. "It's a draft. He wanted to make some sort of restitution since it was his man who was culpable. He said he hoped it would suffice for now."

Adam briefly scanned the paper in the dim light coming through the carriage windows. His eyes widened slightly at the amount on the paper but he said nothing about it, simply folding it and putting it in his waistcoat pocket.

"It was not his responsibility," he commented.

"No, but it salved his pride, I think."

A few minutes passed in silence, each man caught up in his own thoughts.

Dare's mind inevitably turned back to the bride he'd left behind. He was pondering the possibility of a future together when Adam said, "I have some bad news, Dare."

His cousin's tone was so solemn, Dare felt his heart stop. He knew, he just knew, what Adam would say.

"Jenny lost the baby," Dare inserted prosaically.

Adam gave him a startled look. Dare shrugged one

shoulder, a barely perceptible movement that spoke volumes for his rigidly held self-control.

"Dare, Jenny was pregnant with twins. She lost one of them. The other, little Miranda, is fine, if a trifle small." He paused, allowing his words to penetrate before he added, "Your son didn't make it."

Worded in such a way, Dare felt his throat close up. His immediate instinct was to claw at his neck, try to open up his windpipe to let in a desperately needed breath.

But his countenance remained stoic. All the panic was within, threatening to destroy him—as it had been for the past six months.

The baronet continued before he could make his voice work properly.

"There's more," Adam reported with a bone-weary sigh. "Jenny is dying, Dare. Con doesn't know what to do. He said she should be fine but she's declining rapidly. He's at his wit's end. She doesn't seem to want to live."

Dare's expression didn't change one whit. None of his inner panic was revealed in his features or demeanor. None of his affronted anger was displayed either.

In an eerily calm tone, Dare replied, "How dare she? Does she not realize she has a child to care for?"

Adam, owning a perception of which few men could

boast, saw beneath Dare's calm demeanor to the demons lurking within. "It appears," he said carefully, "that she has forgotten that simple fact. Although Con has tried to tell her."

Dare turned his face away, staring out the carriage window. "Spoiled brat," he said conversationally. "She will let my daughter grow up without a mother just because her life has not turned out exactly the way she planned. I'm tempted to go and beat some sense into her."

Considering this threat was uttered in the calmest, most emotionless tone, Adam's reaction might have been viewed as extreme to an outsider.

The baronet's fist slammed into the side of the carriage —right next to his young cousin's face.

Dare didn't really react. He turned, viewed Adam with a trace of disdain, and smiled thinly. "What, may I ask, was the purpose of that?"

"Dammit! Show some life, you soulless cur." Growling, Adam lunged forward, grabbing the front of Dare's coat in one fist. He jerked his cousin out of the seat, bringing his face close. "I know you care. I can feel it in the way you try so hard to look like you don't. If you keep hiding behind that soulless façade of yours, you will snap at the wrong time. Do you really want to hurt Jenny? Or would you rather take a few shots at me?"

The last word had barely left Adam's mouth before Dare's fist smashed into his head. Adam's hand opened, releasing his cousin. The baronet sat back with a pleased smile, absently massaging his ringing ear.

Which only enraged Dare all the more. He launched himself at the other man.

The close proportions of a moving carriage were not conducive to an effective exchange of blows. Adam very easily shoved Dare back in his seat, laughing at the younger man's fury.

"Oh, stubble it, Dare," he said affectionately. "You've had your outlet and I can assure you, I'll be hearing bells for a sennight."

Dare somehow managed to calm the unleashed fury roiling through him. Adam was right; he'd been perilously close to losing all sense where Jenny was concerned.

But, dear God, she was letting herself die! How could she do that to their child?

How could she do that to him?

Not bothering to look at his cousin, he asked, "Are we going to London, then?"

Adam shook his head. "Jenny has been living in a cottage on Denbigh's estate since you left. We go there."

Dare's gaze swung around to meet Adam's. "She left her parents' home?"

Adam nodded. "It was quite a to-do. She calmly told them that she would not live with them and wanted her own house. Denbigh had no choice but to comply. The only ones she was willing to see were Miles and Gwen. She even balked at allowing Con near her after the babies were born." He shrugged a little helplessly, in Dare's opinion. "But now, she doesn't seem to care who is there—or who isn't."

Dare did not miss the significance of his cousin's words. Jenny didn't even care that he wasn't there.

But he suspected that at one time, she had.

Eighteen

Predictably, it was raining. Not a gentle, drizzly rain but a cold, soulless drenching that permeated the bones and made a man wish for nothing more than a cozy armchair before a crackling blaze.

Dare wasn't sure such a thing would even begin to ease the cold he felt. The coach approached Denbigh Castle and he felt nothing so much as the unmistakable longing to flee.

But flight had accomplished naught so far. And, quite frankly, Dare was tired of running.

He'd run from everything. It was not something he was proud of but he'd never really realized it before. Whenever there was the slightest bit of adversity in his life, he'd run. When Adam's offer to go to sea had been raised, Dare had leapt at it. Never had it been so easy to avoid responsibility.

And now, Dare found himself in a situation far worse than any he'd ever experienced before. He was about to see his wife again after nearly six months; the woman he'd fled twice now.

He almost hoped she'd tell him to leave.

The carriage pulled to a stop before the castle. It was not really a castle considering it was a mere century or so old but it looked like one, its impressive façade rising above him like something out of a Gothic novel.

Bloody hell, that was just what he needed. Imagining the home of his wife's family to contain some sort of Gothic tendency was not good for his already unbalanced mind.

He exited the coach and moved to the front steps. The door opened and he was shown into a chamber by a very proper butler to await the duke and Lord Connor.

Dare tried to sit calmly and wait but he was too agitated to be still. He paced over to the fireplace, staring down into the leaping flames. Any answers he may have desired were absent from the mesmerizing blaze. But they did succeed in calming him somewhat.

He turned at the sound of the door. Lord Connor trailed in behind his father, his face appearing to have aged five years in the last few months. Denbigh looked as he ever did. Dare wondered if the man was even human.

"My lords," Dare murmured politely, a small dip of his upper body passing for a barely civil bow.

The duke nodded but said nothing. Dare realized the

man was human after all. His eyes held the haunted quality of a man nearing despair. He was taking his daughter's decline rather hard, then.

Lord Connor gave Dare a long look filled with so many rioting emotions that the younger man had trouble pinpointing just one. He assumed there was a good bit of fury in there as well as panic.

"Have you tried scolding her?" Dare asked, only half-jesting.

Connor's head jerked as if slapped. The duke almost smiled. Dare shrugged his shoulders a bit, adding, "From what I understand, she's acting like a spoiled child. I just thought…"

Dare glanced at Connor and wasn't surprised to see the man's hands clench into fists. His voice was taut with fury. "You know little of the situation, Prestwich, so I would advise that you keep your unwanted suggestions to yourself."

Dare smiled dangerously. "Perhaps I would know a little more had it not been rather ruthlessly pointed out to me that I was not wanted here."

The duke's expression turned rueful. He moved further into the room and seated himself in a chair near the fire, and in so doing, nearer his son-in-law.

He gestured to the other chair. When Dare hesitated, he said, "Indulge me."

Dare dropped his tall frame into the seat, sprawling a bit as was his wont, and watched Connor as he moved another chair closer.

"You have a right to be upset," Lord Denbigh began, shocking Dare to the core of his being. A grunt from the duke's son was disregarded. "We bungled the whole affair badly. We offer our apologies for the pain and misery our actions may have caused."

Dare said nothing for a long while. He just stared at these two men who, with their overwhelming conceit, managed to nearly ruin the lives of two people, one of whom they professed to love. Part of him acknowledged his own guilt and accepted the rightness of their anger.

"You lied to me," he said, ignoring the apology for the nonce.

"I did," Denbigh admitted.

Dare couldn't leave it at that. "Jenny didn't want me to leave. She didn't know anything about it."

The duke nodded, his fingers steepled in front of him. "True. Jenny was most distraught when she realized what had occurred. We tried to find you after the ceremony but you had somehow managed to disappear quite thoroughly."

"I've gotten rather good at disappearing over the years," Dare inserted dryly. Connor's snort of derision was not ignored this time. "Do you have anything intelligent to add to this interview, my lord? Or are you here simply to berate me for my past mistakes?"

Denbigh lifted a hand to intervene in what would probably become an all-out brawl. "Arguing amongst ourselves will not solve this dilemma," he pointed out reasonably. "Jenny is dying, Darius."

Put so bluntly, Dare couldn't respond for a moment. Adam had said the same thing but coming from her father, as it was now, it seemed far worse.

"And Connor had done everything he can for her physically. Nothing seems to help."

"The only time she shows any kind of life is when Lucy brings Miranda in so Jenny can nurse the child," Connor added, his temper firmly under control.

Dare's dark eyes swiveled between the two men. "Who is Lucy?" he asked, selecting the least important tidbit in Connor's revelation.

Connor gaped at him for a moment, at a sudden loss. "I tell you Jenny's dead to the world and you ask about her maid?"

Dare almost smiled at him. "All you had to say was,

'Her maid.' How difficult would that have been?"

"Hell and the devil confound it, Father! He's completely addlebrained. How can she possibly be pining away for him?"

The duke remained silent, almost as if he was nothing more than a mere spectator. His steepled fingers were pressed to his lips and his eyes reflected a tinge of humor at his son's assessment.

Connor emitted a grunt of absolute disgust and rose to his feet. "I refuse to sit here and trade nonsense with you," he told their unwanted guest. "Father can tell you any other unimportant details you want to know." He stormed from the room.

Denbigh watched him go, amused. "I have not seen him so agitated since he was courting his wife," he mused reflectively.

"Does Jenny want to see me, sir?"

The duke's gaze returned to the younger man. "She has never stopped," he admitted quietly. He stared silently at his guest for a moment. Then, leaning forward, he confided, "I cannot tell you how wrong I was to try to manipulate you as I did. I underestimated you and that blasted pride of yours."

An uneasy feeling slid over Dare's spine. "What?"

"I had hoped, that in asking you to leave, that you would defy me by staying. I was stymied when you obeyed."

"You said she didn't want me as husband," Dare pointed out numbly. "Did you believe I was the type to force my presence on an unwilling woman?"

Denbigh sat back with a long sigh. "I chose the wrong words. At the time, I but suspected the depth of my daughter's feelings. You…well, you were a little easier to read, actually."

Dare was fast becoming angry. He hated manipulation and to think that he and Jenny had been the victims this time made him see red.

Holding his emotions firmly in check, he asked, "Where is my brother?"

The duke looked surprised, then suspicious, then resigned. "You are not ready to forgive. You are well matched with my daughter. She has yet to forgive as well."

"Where?"

The older man sighed. "He and Gwen live in the cottage down the lane from Jenny. My coachman will take you there."

Several minutes later, Dare found himself outside a small house, handsomely built in a pleasing setting—or it would have been if the rain was not still making its annoying presence felt. It crossed his mind that his brother might be a gentleman farmer now and he couldn't stop the laugh that escaped.

The door opened before he even reached it. Miles stood there, his face as blank as ever, his eyes glittering with what looked suspiciously like tears. Dare shook his head. It was just the rain, fouling up his sight.

He had reason to reassess his conjecture when his brother reached over the few feet that separated them and dragged him into his arms.

"Thank God you're home," Miles said in the most natural way, just as if Dare belonged there.

And an ache in his chest told Dare more clearly than words that he *wanted* to belong there.

Pushing himself away, he quipped, "So, I hear you are married now?"

Gwen was getting big with child, her radiance a

beacon on this ugly, gray day. Dare wondered if Jenny was so beautiful when she was big with his child. He wished, yet again, that he'd been there to see it.

Miles noticed the direction of his twin's stare. "The midwife predicts twins," he informed him, his normally serious expression softening into amusement.

"Ah," Dare replied, the only word he could manage past the lump in his throat. He raised the glass of whiskey he held, downing it in the vain hope that it would drown the incipient tears he felt burning behind his eyes.

How, he wondered irrelevantly, does one actually *drown* tears?

Miles frowned, motioning to his wife to leave the room. She nodded and rose as gracefully as she was able, leaving the gentlemen to themselves.

Miles leaned forward, not having missed his brother's distress. "Have you been to see her yet?"

Dare silently shook his head. "I am thinking about running again. What do you think?" he said, his mind agreeing violently while his heart threatened to kill him for even thinking such a thing.

"If I thought you were in earnest, I'd be obliged to stop you."

"Indeed," murmured Dare, refilling his whiskey. He

pondered the interesting question of how much it would take to make him oblivious to his own rocky emotions. "I am such a coward!"

The words burst out as if trying to escape, creating a tension in the room that Dare bitterly wished didn't exist.

"You are not a coward, Dare," his brother responded, sincerity positively oozing from his tone.

Dare's grip tightened on his glass. "I run when I'm scared, Miles. What is that if not cowardice?"

Miles did not agree. "You may run but you always come back to face the consequences. What is that if not bravery?"

"Perhaps I should have tried to be more like you," Dare mused, almost to himself. "Father constantly berated me for being such a loose screw, for not having the sense God gave a gnat." He met his brother's eyes. "He told me once that if I was more like you, he'd like me better."

Miles was stupefied. "He always told me I was too stiff-necked and should be more like you, learn to enjoy myself. He constantly berated me for wanting to hide in my books and papers instead of living my life."

The brothers gazed at each other in honest amazement. It had never occurred to them that their father was the reason that they held such resentment for one another.

"Well," Dare muttered finally, quaffing his drink. He refilled the glass and handed it silently to his brother.

Miles accepted the glass, stared at his twin for another moment, then lifted the tumbler and swallowed the amber liquid.

"So much for never drinking," Dare commented dryly.

"Quite," his brother agreed. He handed the glass back, however, and waved away the offer of a refill.

"It's time, Dare," Miles said so quietly that his twin almost didn't hear him.

Inwardly, Dare sighed. Yes, it was time. Part of him rejoiced that he was finally to see the woman he loved after six interminable months without her. The other part rebelled at the inevitable rejection he would receive at her oh so delicate hands. What woman would want a cowardly husband, after all?

"Madam, would you like me to help you dress?"

Jenny barely heard her maid's offer through the dense fog that seemed to have taken up residence in her mind. It was the same offer made every morning. And every morning, Jenny refused, preferring to cocoon herself away in her bed, pretending her life was not what it was.

How could she have come to this pass? Her husband preferred his travels to her. Her baby boy died in her arms. Her baby girl did nothing but cry. And she felt so lost and so alone that she couldn't even dredge up a modicum of her innate pride to rescue her from complete mental breakdown.

It was too much to be borne!

Something in Jenny snapped. She was unsure if that something actually broke or if it had actually somehow righted itself in her numbed brain. She didn't care.

Raising herself up on her weakened arms, she nodded to Lucy. "Yes, Lucy, I do believe I will dress today."

Nineteen

Jenny sat in a rocking chair in the little room just off her own. It was this room that sheltered her child, the precious, beautiful little girl with black hair and pale blue eyes. Jenny cradled the infant to her breast, suckling the baby and crooning meaningless little words that meant the entire world to the child, as she rocked back and forth.

Miranda made soft little sounds of contentment as she released her mother's breast and yawned sleepily. Jenny adjusted her clothing and continued rocking her baby, marveling at such perfection. How could she have been so selfish as to ignore this perfect little girl?

Her heart would always ache for her baby boy, the little being who should have been there to be raised as his father's heir.

A choking sob caught in her throat. She held it back, refusing to cry anymore. As if discerning her suffering, Miranda fussed, clenching and unclenching her tiny fists.

Jenny sensed another presence intruding. Glancing up

briefly, she saw her brother-in-law leaning against the doorpost and frowned, returning her gaze to her daughter. "Good morning, Miles," she said absently. When he didn't respond, she looked up again, her eyes narrowed in question.

Her heart stopped beating for a long moment then picked up faster than before.

Dare.

His dark brows were raised in amusement. She saw the smile in his eyes and the one on his lips. His long hair was pulled back, as usual. His arms were crossed over his chest and he appeared utterly at ease.

Jenny sensed the coiled tension in him, however. He was unsure of his reception, she realized, and was bracing himself for her rejection.

Rising slowly so as not to disturb her sleeping child, Jenny moved to the bassinet near the window. She very carefully set the baby down, maintaining abnormal control over her suddenly trembling body.

Not even looking up, Jenny brushed right by her husband. She could feel him watching her but she didn't care.

Feeling as though her heart was breaking and not exactly sure why, Jenny retreated to her bedchamber.

Dare was astounded by the change in his wife. She had always been rather delicate but now she was nearly skeletal —far too thin for a woman who'd recently given birth to twins.

In fact, her entire appearance had suffered in her decline. Her unbound hair was dull and her pale blue eyes seemed almost lifeless in her gaunt face.

He made to follow her but the unwelcome thought intruded that perhaps she would not want him to. He hesitated one second before brushing the thought firmly aside.

She was in her room, seated at her dressing table, dragging a brush through her long blond curls. He stepped up behind her and gently removed the brush from her trembling fingers.

He took over the task, not speaking. She kept her eyes downcast, and twisted her hands together in her lap but she didn't stop him as he half expected her to do.

Dare watched her face and watched the brush in his hand as it glided through her hair. He'd dreamed often of her hair, spread over his pillow, lying on her shoulders, masking her naked breasts. He'd dreamed of her so often that his fantasies had merged with his reality causing him no end of melancholy and physical discomfort.

He glanced in the mirror again to find her watching him, the expression in her cornflower eyes unreadable. But he sensed her pain and knew he was the cause no matter what her father had done to precipitate his flight.

He set the brush aside and crouched down beside her stool. Taking her chilled hand in his own, he tried to smile. He was afraid it more closely resembled a grimace, however.

"Jenny-love, we have to talk," he told her, his voice breaking slightly on his pet name for her. He cursed under his breath and firmly reined in his disturbing emotions.

He wasn't sure she'd answer. When she did, her words sliced through his heart, threatening to bleed him dry.

"Why did you leave?"

He sucked in a harsh breath, his fingers tightening involuntarily. "Your father said you wanted me to go," he said woodenly.

"After all we've shared, how could you believe I would want you to go?"

All the hurt, the feelings of abandonment, and betrayal were painfully clear in her voice. Dare reacted instinctively, pressing his lips to her bare knuckles with a reverence he'd never felt for another woman.

"I was stupidly proud, my love," he admitted in a whisper. "Too proud, too frightened of the possibility that it was true to even consider asking you. My damnable pride, something I have not suffered from for more years than I can count, decided to rear its blasted head." He curved his free hand over her cheek, feeling the wetness of her tears. "I am not making excuses, Jenny. I am truly sorry for the pain I've caused you."

Jenny's eyes fluttered open and he thought he just might drown in those azure depths.

The moment had come. Dare could no longer avoid it. He had to tell her what was in his heart, what made him breathe, what kept him sane.

So he did.

"I love you, Jenny. With all my heart and soul, with every breath in my body, with all my being. I wish to spend my life proving to you how important you are to me and how sorry I am for forcing you through so much hell."

Jenny's fingers tightened on his. Her lips twisted into a small smile, which grew as she replied, "Only if you allow me the same privilege, my dearest love."

At his questioning look, Jenny released a tinkling

laugh. "I could have hunted you down, you know. I could have told you long ago how I felt. I didn't want to burden you and make you feel obligated to me. It was my pride that made me refuse to debase myself by pouring out my heart when I wasn't sure what it was you felt for me."

"None of this was your fault," he insisted, in true gentlemanly fashion.

Jenny laid her hand against his stubbled jaw. "As I took part of the blame for my pregnancy, I take part of the blame for every contretemps we've gotten into from the start. We've neither one of us behaved very admirably this past year, Dare."

He would have refuted her words but she placed a gentle finger over his lips, silencing his protest.

"And so, I ask that you allow me the same privilege you have requested. To love you with my whole heart, soul, and being, 'til my dying breath. And to spend my life proving to you how important you are to me and how sorry I am for causing you so much needless suffering. I am truly sorry, Dare. I never meant to add more pain to your already tormented past."

"Oh, Jenny-love, you have no idea how I needed to hear you say that." He wrapped his arms around her, laying his head against her chest, a sigh of deep relief echoing through his body and into hers.

She smiled as she stroked her fingers through his silky, black hair. "My admission that I caused your pain?" she asked facetiously.

She felt him smile against her belly, the movement causing familiar flutters of sensation quivering all through her body.

"No, that you love me. You could tell me that every minute of every day for the rest of our lives and I would never get tired of hearing it."

"Then you'll stay?" She asked tentatively but with such a vast amount of hope that he was momentarily too choked up to reply. After taking a deep breath, he smiled, saying, "Aye, Jenny-love. Of course I'll stay."

Taking his head in her hands, Jenny leaned down. Her lips pressed sweetly to his, her innocence despite being a mother charming him all over again.

They rose as one and he pressed her full-length against him, an action she aided by moving so close he thought she just might be trying to disappear under his skin.

He swung her up into his arms, intent on her bed on the other side of the room when a sudden thought occurred to him.

"Is it too soon?"

Jenny smiled with true joy for the first time since their wedding. She shook her head, a laugh escaping when his pace quickened.

An hour later, Dare leaned up on his elbow, absently fondling a lock of his wife's hair. She stared up at him, her dazed expression the highest compliment she could have paid him. He smiled and leaned down to place a soft kiss on her slightly parted lips.

She sighed when he moved back. "That was beautiful," she breathed.

He laughed. "A rather lukewarm description but I'll accept it as a compliment," he said.

Jenny lightly slapped him. "I meant the kiss, you looby. The other was"—she blushed and released a little contented sigh—"earth-shattering."

He rewarded her for that with a deep, soul-stealing kiss that left her weak in the knees and begging for more.

An infantile cry from the next room interrupted their loveplay. Dare lifted his head, his face freezing at the sound. He'd forgotten their child. How could he forget his own daughter?

"Miranda," he whispered, his dark-eyed gaze fixed on the door opposite.

Jenny smiled, her white teeth flashing. "Would you like to meet your daughter?" she asked.

He breathed the word, "Yes."

Jenny rose and drew on a sapphire blue silk dressing gown. After shooting him an utterly seductive, utterly endearing grin, she disappeared into the baby's room.

Dare sat up and pulled on his breeches. He sat there for a moment, nearly lost in thought, before dragging his fingers through his hair and tying it back with one of Jenny's ribbons. He didn't bother with anything else.

He was at the door only seconds after Jenny's departure, gazing into the room that held his wife and daughter, the two most precious beings in his world.

His bride turned at his entrance, a serene smile in her beautiful eyes and an invitation to join them on her perfect lips.

Dare approached cautiously, more nervous than he could ever remember being in his life. He carefully blanked his expression, not wanting to alarm Jenny and unsure of the amount of fear a child could sense. His bride handed Miranda over, calmly confident in his nonexistent knowledge of babies. Her attitude helped calm him... a bit.

Dare took his daughter into his arms, cradling her tight to his bare chest. When he looked down into the palest blue eyes and smelled that sweet baby smell, something in him cracked.

Gazing down at his child with fascinated awe, the young father moved away from his wife. He started whispering words of love and devotion to the child, not even bothered by the fact that his behavior was not in keeping with how their class operated.

This child, this bright spot in his life, was worth more to him than any ridiculous strictures imposed by a Society that encouraged infidelity, hypocrisy, and every other vice known to man.

This child…and his wife.

His beautiful, strong, willful wife, with her mistaken beliefs and humorous tendencies. She loved him when no one else did and refused to see him as anything other than a man worthy of her tender regard, someone worth redeeming. And while Dare hesitated, even now, to agree with her assessment, he couldn't help but love her for the belief he'd always craved but never hoped to receive.

Jenny watched her husband with love, hunger, and an odd twinge of pain. He was so obviously in love with his daughter that Jenny fell in love with him all over again. It was distressing how much time they had lost due to their stupid pride.

As if sensing her disquieting thoughts, Dare looked up, meeting her eyes. His own looked rather wet. Jenny smiled hesitantly feeling the sting of tears and not even bothering to stem the flow.

Dare's expression was no longer blank. He stared at her with all the love in his heart and soul. Then, whispering so low that she had to lean forward to hear, he said, "Thank you."

The End

About the Author

Jaimey Grant, a pseudonym for Laura Miller, was born in Michigan in 1979. After a fun-filled childhood interlaced with moments of emotional trauma and an insatiable curiosity about the reasons people act the way they do, she became a writer.

Primarily a Regency romance author, Jaimey has also dabbled in fantasy of a non-romance variety. A comprehensive list of works and where to find them can be found on her website, www.jaimeygrant.com. There are more Regencies and fantasies in the works.

She currently lives in Michigan with her husband and two children.

To learn more about Jaimey and her work, visit any of the sites below.

Website: http://www.jaimeygrant.com
Blog: http://jaimeygrant.blogspot.com
Facebook: http://www.facebook.com/jaimeygrantauthor
Email: jaimeygrant@yahoo.com